W9-CNO-682

www.MinotaurBooks.com

The premier website for the best in crime fiction

Log on and learn more about:

The Labyrinth: Sign up for this monthly newsletter and get your crime fiction fix. Commentary author Q&A, hot new titles, and giveaways.

MomentsInCrime: It's no mystery what our authors are thinking. Each week, a new author blogs about their upcoming projects, special events, and more. Log on today to talk to your favorite authors.
www.MomentsInCrime.com

GetCozy: The ultimate cozy connection. Find your favorite cozy mystery, grab a reading group guide, sign up for monthly giveaways, and more.
www.GetCozyOnline.com

THE WALKERS OF DEMBLEY

"British cozy fans will no doubt find this book an engaging teatime companion."   —*Booklist*

"Trenchant and droll."   —*St. Petersburg Times*

"Among writers of cozy village mystery series, count M.C. Beaton as one who creates a nice tea party."
          —Associated Press

THE POTTED GARDENER

"From the author's sure-fire plot comes this fail-safe moral: It takes an outsider to open people's eyes to the beauty—and the evil—within."
          —*The New York Times Book Review*

"Compare this one to lemon meringue pie: light. . .with a delicious hint of tartness at its heart."
          —*Washington Times*

A SPOONFUL OF POISON

"Agatha is like Miss Marple with a drinking problem, pack-a-day habit, and major man lust...Beaton's latest installment, in which Aggie gets mixed up in a deadly jam-tasting contest, is pretty terrific—a must-read."
          —*Entertainment Weekly*

"Take two fine old English traditions—the village fete and death by poison—and you have a clever tale…featuring irascible, lovable Agatha Raisin. *A Spoonful of Poison* will go down just fine."

—*Richmond Times-Dispatch*

"Beaton's sly humor enhances the cozy-style plotting, while updates on Agatha's…romantic travails are as delightful as ever. The open-ended resolution points to more madcap mayhem to come."   —*Publishers Weekly*

KISSING CHRISTMAS GOODBYE

"Agatha Raisin is still at the top of her game…in her most challenging case yet."   —*Publishers Weekly*

"Beaton, the reigning queen of the cozies, adds an English manor house and a Christmas theme to her usual Cotswold village setting, upping the comfiness factor even higher."   —*Booklist*

LOVE, LIES AND LIQUOR

"Another highly satisfying Beaton cozy, this one is long on the kind of social comedy that uses character, plot, and atmosphere to produce the laughter."   —*Booklist*

"Driven by Agatha's strong personality, [*Love, Lies and Liquor*] will please devoted fans."   —*Publishers Weekly*

Also By M. C. Beaton

AGATHA RAISIN

A Spoonful of Poison
Kissing Christmas Goodbye
Love, Lies and Liquor
The Perfect Paragon
The Deadly Dance
Agatha Raisin and the Haunted House
Agatha Raisin and the Case of the Curious Curate
Agatha Raisin and the Day the Floods Came
Agatha Raisin and the Love from Hell
Agatha Raisin and the Fairies of Fryfam
Agatha Raisin and the Witch of Wyckhadden
Agatha Raisin and the Wizard of Evesham
Agatha Raisin and the Wellspring of Death
Agatha Raisin and the Terrible Tourist
Agatha Raisin and the Murderous Marriage
The Potted Gardener
The Vicious Vet
The Quiche of Death

The Skeleton in the Closet

HAMISH MACBETH

Death of a Bore
Death of a Poison Pen
Death of a Village
Death of a Celebrity
A Highland Christmas

WRITING AS MARION CHESNEY

Our Lady of Pain
Sick of Shadows
Hasty Death
Snobbery with Violence

THE WALKERS
OF DEMBLEY

An Agatha Raisin Mystery

M. C. Beaton

St. Martin's Paperbacks

This is a work of fiction. All of the characters, organizations, and events portrayed in this novel are either products of the author's imagination or are used fictitiously.

THE WALKERS OF DEMBLEY

Copyright © 1995 by M. C. Beaton.
Excerpt from *A Spoonful of Poison* copyright © 2008 by M. C. Beaton.

For information address St. Martin's Press, 175 Fifth Avenue, New York, NY 10010.

Library of Congress Catalog Card Number: 94-44492

ISBN: 0-312-53913-4
EAN: 978-0-312-53913-9

Printed in the United States of America

St. Martin's hardcover edition / April 1994
Ballantine Ivy edition / December 1996
St. Martin's Paperbacks edition / August 2009

St. Martin's Paperbacks are published by St. Martin's Press, 175 Fifth Avenue, New York, NY 10010.

10 9 8 7 6 5 4 3 2 1

ONE

✝

AGATHA Raisin watched the sunlight on the wall of her office in the City of London.

It was shining through the slats on the venetian blind, long arrows of light inching down the wall as the sun sank lower, the sundial of Agatha's working day.

Tomorrow it would all be over, her stint as a public-relations officer, and then she could return to her home in the village of Carsely in the Cotswolds. She had not enjoyed her return to work. Her short time away from it, her short time in retirement, had seemed to divorce her from the energy required to drum up publicity for clients from journalists and television companies.

Although she had enough of her old truculence and energy left to make a success of it, she missed the village and her friends. She had gone back initially for a few weekends when she could get away, but the wrench of returning to London had been so great that for the past two months she had stayed where she was, working at the weekends as well.

She had thought that her new-found talent for making friends would have worked for her in the City, but most of the staff were young compared to her fifty-something and preferred to congregate together at lunch-time and after work. Roy Silver, her young friend who had inveigled her into working for Pedmans for six months, also had been steering clear of her of late, always claiming he was "too busy" to meet her for a drink or even to talk to her.

She sighed and looked at the clock. She was taking a journalist from the *Daily Bugle* out for drinks and dinner to promote a new pop star, Jeff Loon, real name Trevor Biles, and she was not looking forward to it. It was hard to promote someone like Jeff Loon, a weedy, acne-pitted youth with a mouth like a sewer. But he had a voice which used to be described as Irish parlour tenor and had recently re-recorded some old romantic favourites, all great hits. It was necessary then to give him a new image as the darling of middle England, the kind that the mums and dads adored. The best way was to keep him away from the press as much as possible and send in Agatha Raisin.

She went to the staff bathroom and changed into a black dress and pearls, suitable to foster the staid image of the client she was representing. The journalist she was to meet was new to her. She had checked up on him. His name was Ross Andrews. He had once been a major-league reporter but had been demoted to the entertainments page in middle age. Ageing journalists often found themselves relegated to reporting on the social or entertainments page or, worse, to answering readers' letters.

They were to meet in the City, Fleet Street being no more, the newspaper companies having moved down to the East End.

She had agreed to meet Ross in the bar of the City Hotel and to eat there as well, for the restaurant was passable and its windows commanded a good view of the river Thames.

She twisted this way and that in front of the mirror. The dress, a recent purchase, looked suspiciously tight. Too many expense-account dinners and lunches. As soon as she got back to Carsely, she would take the weight off.

As she walked down to the entrance hall, the doorman, Jock, sprang to open the door. "Good night, Mrs. Raisin," he said with an oily smile, and muttered under his breath once Agatha was out of earshot, "Rotten old bat!" For Agatha had once snapped at him, "If you're a doorman, then open the bloody door every time you see me. Hop to it!" and the lazy Jock had never forgiven her.

Agatha walked along with the thinning home-going crowds, a stocky, pugnacious woman with a short hairstyle, bearlike eyes, and good legs.

The hotel was only a few streets away. She left the evening sunlight and plunged into the gloom of the hotel bar. Although she had never met this Ross Andrews before, her experienced eye picked him out immediately. He was wearing a dark suit and a collar and tie, but he had that raffish seediness about him of a newspaper journalist. He had thinning hair of a suspicious black, a fat face with a smudge of a nose and watery-blue eyes. He might have once been good-looking, thought Agatha as she walked towards him, but years of heavy boozing had taken their toll.

"Mr. Andrews?"

"Mrs. Raisin. Call me Ross. I ordered a drink and put it on your tab," he said cheerfully. "It's all on expenses anyway."

3

Agatha reflected that quite a number of journalists were expert at putting in fake restaurant bills for clients they should have entertained and never did, pocketing the money themselves. But when it came to anyone else's expenses, it seemed to be a case of no holds barred.

She nodded and sat down opposite him, signalled to the waiter and ordered a gin and tonic for herself. "Call me Agatha," she said.

"How are things on the *Daily Bugle*?" asked Agatha, knowing that it was pointless talking business until the journalist considered he had sunk enough booze to warrant a few lines.

"On the skids, if you ask me," he said gloomily. "The trouble is that these new journalists don't know their arses from their elbows. They come out of these damn schools of journalism and they're not a patch on the likes of us who had to learn to fly by the seat of our pants. Come back off a job and say, 'Oh, I couldn't ask him or her that. Husband just dead,' or some crap like that. I say to them, 'Laddie, in my day, we got it on the front page and the hell with anyone's feelings.' They want to be *liked*. A good reporter is *never* liked."

"True," agreed Agatha with some feeling.

He signalled the waiter and ordered himself another whisky and water without asking Agatha if she was ready for another drink.

"It all happened when they turned the running of the newspapers over to accountants, seedy jealous bods who cut your expenses and argue about every penny. Why, I remember . . ."

Agatha smiled and tuned him out. How many times had she been in similar circumstances, listening to similar

4

complaints? Tomorrow she would be free and she would never go back to work again, not as a PR anyway. She had sold her own PR firm to take early retirement, to retire to the Cotswolds, to the village of Carsely, which had slowly enfolded her in its gentle warmth. She missed it. She missed the Carsely Ladies Society, the chatter over the teacups in the vicarage, the placid life of the village. Keeping a practised look of admiration on her face as Ross wittered on, her thoughts moved to her neighbour, James Lacey. She had had a drink with him on her last visit to the village but their easy friendship seemed to have gone. She told herself that her silly obsession for him had fled, never to return. Still, they had had fun solving those murders.

As Ross raised his arm to order another drink, she forestalled him by suggesting firmly that they should eat.

They walked into the dining-room. "Your usual table, Mrs. Raisin," said the maître d', showing them to a table at the window.

There had been a time, reflected Agatha, when being known and recognized by maître d's was gratifying, underlying how far she had come from the Birmingham slum in which she had grown up. No one said "slum" these days, of course. It was Inner City, as if the euphemism could take away the grime, violence, and despair. The do-gooders chattered on about poverty but no one was starving, apart from old-age pensioners who were not tough enough to demand benefits owing to them. It was a poverty of the very soul, where imagination was fed by violent videos, drink and drugs.

"And old Chalmers said to me when I came back from Beirut, 'you're too wiley and tough a bird, Ross, to get kidnapped.'"

5

"Absolutely," said Agatha. "What would you like to drink?"

"Mind if I choose? I find the ladies know nothing about wine," which Agatha translated into meaning that the ladies might order inexpensive wine, or half a bottle, or something unacceptable. She thought, he will choose the second most expensive wine, being greedy but not wanting to appear so, and he did. Like some of his ilk, he ordered in the way of food what he thought was due to his position rather than because he enjoyed the taste of it. He did not eat much of it, obviously longing for the brandy at the end of the meal and for someone to take all the expensive muck away. So he barely ate snails, followed by rack of lamb, followed by profiteroles.

Over the brandies, Agatha wearily got down to business. She described Jeff Loon as a nice boy, "too nice for the pop world," who was devoted to his mother and two brothers. She described his forthcoming release. She handed over photographs and press handouts.

"This is a load of shit, you know," said Ross, smiling at her blearily. "I mean, I checked up on this Jeff Loon and he's got a record, and I mean *criminal* record. He's been found guilty on two counts of actual bodily harm and he's also been done for taking drugs, so why are you peddling this crap about him being a mother's boy?"

The pleasant middle-aged woman that had been his impression of Agatha Raisin disappeared and a hard-featured woman with eyes like gimlets faced him.

"And you cut the crap, sweetie," growled Agatha. "You know damn well why you were invited here. If you had no intention of writing anything even half decent, then you shouldn't have come, you greedy pig. I'll tell you something else: I don't give a sod what you write. I just never want to see your like again. You chomp and swig like the failed journalist you are, boring the knickers off me with apocryphal stories of your greatness, and then you have the cheek to say that Jeff is a phony. What about you?"

"Oh, it's not on for PRs to complain, but hear this! I'm going to break the mould. Your editor is going to hear all your stories, verbatim, and get it along with the price of this evening."

"He'll never listen to you!" said Ross.

She fished under the napkin on her lap and held up a small but serviceable tape recorder. "Smile," said Agatha. "You're on candid camera."

He gave a weak laugh. "Aggie, *Aggie.*" He covered her hand with his own. "Can't you take a joke? Of course I'm going to write a nice piece on Jeff."

Agatha signalled for the bill. "I couldn't care less what you write," she said. Ross Andrews had sobered rapidly. "Look, Aggie . . ."

"Agatha to you, but Mrs. Raisin will do now that we've got to know each other so well."

"Look, I promise you a good piece."

Agatha signed the credit-card slip. "You'll get the tape when I read it," she said. She got to her feet. "Good night, Mr. Andrews."

Ross Andrews swore under his breath. Public relations! He hoped never to meet anyone like Agatha Raisin again. He felt quite tearful. Oh, for the days when women were women!

Far away in the heart of Gloucestershire in the market town of Dembley, Jeffrey Benson, seated in the back of a schoolroom which was used for the weekly meeting of the rambling association, the Dembley Walkers, was thinking pretty much the same thing as he watched his lover, Jessica Tartinck, address the group. This feminist business was all very well, and God knew he was all for the equality of women, but why did they have to dress and go on like men?

Jessica was wearing jeans and a workman's shirt hanging loose. She had a pale scholarly face—she held a first in English from Oxford—and thick black hair worn long and straight. She had superb breasts, large and firm. She was rather thick about the thighs and did not have very good legs, but then the legs were always in trousers. Like Jeff, she was a schoolteacher at the local comprehensive. Before she had somehow declared herself leader of the Dembley Walkers, they had been a chatty, inoffensive group of people who enjoyed their weekend rambles.

But Jessica seemed to delight in confrontations with landowners, whom she hated like poison. She was a frequent visitor to the Records Office in Gloucester, poring over maps, finding rights of way which, buried in the mists of time, now had crops planted over them.

Jessica, on arriving to teach at the school a few months before, had immediately looked around for A Cause. She often thought in capital letters. She had learned of the Dembley Walkers through a fellow teacher, a timid, fair-haired girl called Deborah Camden who taught physics. All at once Jessica had found her cause, and in no time at all, without any of the other ramblers' knowing quite how it had happened, she had taken over. That her zeal in finding rights of way for them across private land was fuelled by bitterness and envy and, as in a case of her previous "protests"—she had been an anti-nuclear campaigner on Greenham Common—by a desire for power over people, never crossed her mind. Jessica could find no fault in Jessica, and this was her great strength. She exuded confidence. It was politically incorrect to disagree with her. As most of the genuine ramblers who just wanted a peaceful outing had left and been replaced by ones in Jessica's image, she found it easy to hold sway. Among her most devout admirers, apart from Deborah, was Mary Trapp, a thin, morose girl with bad skin and very, very large feet. Then there was Kelvin Hamilton, a professional Scot who wore a kilt at all times and made jokes about "saxpence," claimed to have come from a Highland village but actually came from Glasgow. There was Alice Dewhurst, a large powerful woman with a large powerful backside, who had known Jessica during the Greenham Common days. Alice's friend, Gemma Queen, a thin, anaemic shop-girl, did not say much except to agree with everything Alice said. Lastly were two men, Peter Hatfield and Terry Brice, who worked at the Copper Kettle Restaurant in Dembley as waiters. Both were thin and quiet, both effeminate, both given to whispering jokes to each other and sniggering.

Jessica looked particularly attractive that evening because she had found fresh prey. There was an old right of way across the land of a baronet, Sir Charles Fraith. She herself had surveyed the territory. There were crops growing across the right of way. She had written to Sir Charles herself to say that they would be marching across his land the Saturday after next and that there was nothing he could do about it.

Deborah suddenly found her hand shooting up. "Yes, Deborah?" asked Jessica, raising thin black eyebrows.

"C-couldn't we j-just once," stammered Deborah,

"j-just go for a walk like we used to? It was fun when old Mr. Jones used to lead us. We had picnics and things and . . ."

Her voice trailed away before the supercilious expression on Jessica's face.

"Come, now, Deborah, this is not like you. If it weren't for rambling groups like ours, there wouldn't be rights of way *at all*."

One of the original pre-Jessica ramblers, Harry Southern, said suddenly, "She's got a point. We're going back to farmer Stone's land this Saturday. He chased us off with a shotgun a month ago and some of the ladies were frightened."

"You mean *you* were frightened," said Jessica haughtily. "Very well. We will put it to a vote. Do we go to farmer Stone's this weekend or not?"

As her acolytes outnumbered the others, the vote was easily carried. Even Deborah no longer had the courage to protest, and after the meeting, when Jessica put an arm around her shoulders and gave her a hug, she felt her doubts ebbing away and all her usual slavish devotion returning.

POETS day in the City, the acronym standing for Piss Off Early Tomorrow's Saturday, had arrived at last. Agatha Raisin cleared her desk. She had an almost childish desire to erase all the telephone numbers of contacts on the Filofax to make it harder for whoever replaced her, but managed to restrain herself. Outside her door, she could hear her secretary singing a happy tune. Agatha had gone through three secretaries during her short stay. The present one, Bunty Dunton, was a big jolly county girl with a skin like a rhinoceros, and so Agatha's often virulent outbursts

10

of temper had seemingly left her untouched. But she had never sounded so happy before.

But it would be all right when she returned to Carsely, thought Agatha. She was popular there.

Her office door opened and Roy Silver edged in. His hair was slicked back with gel and now worn in a pony-tail. He had a spot on his chin and his suit was of the type where the jacket appears to be hanging off the shoulders and the sleeves are turned back at the cuff. His silk tie was broad and a mixture of violent fluorescent colours which seemed to heighten the unhealthy pallor of his face.

"Off then?" he asked, looking poised for flight.

"Oh, sit down, Roy," said Agatha. "I've been here six months and we've hardly seen anything of each other."

"Been busy, you know that, Aggie. So have you. How did you get on with the Jeff Loon account?"

"All right," said Agatha uneasily. She was beginning to wonder why she had gone over the top like that. Not that she had actually taped the creep. She just happened to have had her tape recorder in her handbag and had taken it out while he was absorbed in bragging about himself and put it on her lap under her napkin to trick him.

Roy sat down. "So you're off to Carsely. Look, Aggie, I think you've found your niche."

"You mean PR? Forget it."

"No, I meant Carsely. You're a much easier person to know when you're there."

"What d'you mean?" demanded Agatha truculently. She held up a silver paper-knife she had been about to drop into a box on her desk along with her other belongings. Roy cringed but said firmly, "Well, Aggie, I must say you've been a success, back on your old form, rule by fear and all

11

that. I'd got used to Village Aggie, all tea and crumpets and the doings of the neighbours. Funny, even murder in your parish didn't bring out the beast in you quite the way PR has done."

"I don't indulge in personality clashes," said Agatha, feeling a tide of red starting at her neck and moving up to her face.

"No?" Roy was feeling bolder now. She hadn't thrown anything at him. "Well, what about your seccies, love? Darting along to personnel in floods of tears and sobbing their little hearts out on Mr. Burnham's thirty-four-inch chest. What about that rag-trade queen, Emma Roth?"

"What about her? I got a spread on her in the *Telegraph*."

"But you told the old bat she had the manners of a pig and her fashions were shoddy."

"So she has, and so they are. And did she cancel her account with us? No."

Roy squirmed. "Don't like to see you like this. Get back to Carsely, there's a love, and leave all this nasty London behind. I'm only telling you for your own good."

"Why is it," said Agatha evenly, "that people who say they are only telling you things for your own good come out with a piece of bitchery?"

"Well, we *were* friends once . . ." Roy darted for the door and made his escape.

Agatha stared at the door through which he had disappeared, her mouth a little open. His last remark had dismayed her. The new Agatha surely *made* friends, not lost them. She had blamed London and London life for her loneliness, never stopping to think that by sinking back into her old ways, she had once more started alienating people.

12

There was a separate box on her desk, full of cosmetics and scent, products of her various clients. She had been going to take it home. She called out, "Bunty, come in here a moment."

Her secretary bounced in, fresh face, no make-up, ankle-length white cotton skirt and bare feet. "Here," said Agatha, pushing the box forward, "you can have this stuff."

"Gosh, thanks awfully," said Bunty. "Too kind. Got everything packed, Mrs. Raisin?"

"Just a few more things."

There was something lost and vulnerable in Agatha's bearlike eyes. She was still thinking of what Roy had said.

"Tell you what," said Bunty, "I've brought my little car up to town today. When you're ready, I'll give you a run to Paddington Station."

"Thank you," said Agatha humbly.

And so Agatha, unusually silent and not back-seat driving one bit, was taken to Paddington Station by Bunty. "I live in the Cotswolds," volunteered Bunty. "Of course, I only get home at weekends. Lovely place. We're over in Bibury. You're near Moreton-in-Marsh. If I'm home during the week, I go with Ma to the market on Tuesday." And so she rattled on while all the whole time Agatha kept thinking of how lonely her stay in London had been and how easy it would have been to make a friend of this secretary.

As Agatha got out of the car at Paddington, she said, "You have my address, Bunty. If you ever feel like dropping over for a meal, or just coffee, please do."

"Thanks," said Bunty. "See you."

Agatha trudged onto the train, taking up the seat next to her with her boxes. When the train moved out, gaining

13

speed, and London fell away behind her, Agatha took a long slow breath. She was leaving that other Agatha behind.

Carsley again. After a long dreary winter and a cold wet spring, the sun was blazing down, and Lilac Lane, where Agatha had her cottage, was living up to its name, heavy with blossom of white, mauve, and purple. She saw James Lacey's car parked outside his house and her heart lifted. She admitted to herself that she had missed him—along with everyone else in Carsley, she told herself sternly. Her cleaner, Doris Simpson, who had been caring for Agatha's two cats while she had been away, had been looking out for her, and came out on the step with a smile of welcome.

"Home again, Agatha," she said. "Coffee's ready, and I got a nice piece of steak in for your dinner."

"Thank you, Doris," said Agatha. She stood back a moment and looked affectionately at her cottage, squatting there like a friendly beast under its heavy roof of thatch. Then she went indoors to a chilly reception from her cats, who in their catlike way would not stoop to any raptures on the return of an owner who should have had more consideration than to go away.

Doris carried Agatha's boxes in and put them in the small hall and then went through to the kitchen and poured Agatha a cup of coffee.

"I forgot about the garden," said Agatha. "Must be a right mess."

"Oh, no, the Ladies Society took it in turns to do a bit of weeding, and that Mr. Lacey did quite a bit. Why, what's the matter, Agatha?"

For Agatha had begun to cry.

14

Agatha took out a serviceable handkerchief and blew her nose loudly. "I'm glad to be home," she mumbled.

"It's London," said Doris, nodding her head wisely. "London never did folks any good at all. Me and Bert go up now and then to the shops. It's all crowds and push. Glad to get back to where it's quiet."

The cleaner tactfully turned away until Agatha had composed herself.

"So what's been going on in the village?" asked Agatha.

"Not much, I'm glad to say. Reckon as how us is in for a nice quiet time. Oh, there's a new thing. We've got a ramblers' group."

"Who's running that?"

"Mr. Lacey."

Agatha was suddenly conscious of the expense-account rolls of fat around her middle. "I'd like to join. How do I go about it?"

"Don't think anyone *joins,* 'zactly. Us meets up outside Harvey's after lunch on Sunday, about half past one. Mr. Lacey takes us on one of the countryside walks and tells us about the plants and things and a bit o' the history. Lived here all my life and the things I don't know!"

"No trouble with the landowners?"

"Not around here. Lord Pendlebury's people keep the walks nice and neat, and signposted, too. We did have a bit of trouble over at Mr. Jackson's." Mr. Jackson owned a chain of computer shops and had bought a large piece of land. "We was following the marked path and came up against a padlocked gate right across it and there was Harry Cater, Jackson's agent, with a shotgun, telling us to get off the land."

15

"He can't do that!"

"No, but Mr. Lacey said with so many nice places around, it wasn't worth the trouble making a fuss. Miss Simms, she told Cater what to do with his shotgun and where to put it, and with the vicar and his wife listening and all. I didn't know where to look."

"Rambling," said Agatha thoughtfully. "Now there's a thing." This was Friday. On Sunday she would see James again if she did not run him to earth before then.

Roy Silver walked into Mr. Wilson's office the following morning, wondering why he had been summoned to work on a Saturday.

Mr. Wilson, the boss of Pedmans, was sitting with a copy of the *Daily Bugle* spread on his desk in front of him.

"Seen the paper this morning?" he asked.

"The *Daily Bugle*? No, not yet."

"Our Mrs. Raisin has turned up trumps again. Lovely piece about Jeff Loon, worth thousands in free publicity. My God, if she can promote a pillock like Jeff Loon, she can promote anything. He was your account and we turned it over to Mrs. Raisin when you weren't getting anywhere with it."

"Well, no one wanted to know," said Roy defensively.

Mr. Wilson looked at Roy over the top of his gold-rimmed glasses.

"I'm not blaming you. I don't think anyone else in PR could have pulled off a coup like this." He leaned back in his chair. "I thought you and Mrs. Raisin were best friends."

"So we are."

"I noticed you seemed to avoid her while she was here.

16

I overheard her asking you to go for a drink with her after work one day, and heard you coming out with the lamest of excuses."

"Must have heard the wrong thing. I adore Aggie."

"You see, I want you to get close to that woman. I want you to talk to her about money, lots of money. I'll even make her a partner. She can choose her own accounts. She doesn't like me. If there's any affection left between you . . ."

"Lots," said Roy fervently.

"Okay, get down there. Take your time. Don't rush her. Look for a way to get her back."

"Maybe next weekend?"

"Nothing up with the present."

"Of course, of course. I'll go now."

Roy rushed off home to pack a weekend bag and then took a taxi to Paddington. He had not phoned Agatha, fearing she would suggest another weekend or put him off altogether. If he just arrived on the doorstep, so he reasoned, she could hardly turn him away.

Had James Lacey been in the Red Lion that Saturday evening, which is where Roy finally ran Agatha to earth, then she might have told Roy to get lost. But the thought of seeing James again on the Sunday was filling her with nervous anticipation. To have even the weedy Roy along might mean she would not be tempted to monopolize him. So she ungraciously said, "I am surprised an *ex-friend* should be so anxious to stay with me, but I suppose I'll have to put up with you putting up with me. Prepare for an energetic day tomorrow. In fact, it'll probably bore the pants off you and serve you right. Tomorrow morning we go to church, and

17

after that we join the Carsely Ramblers for a long and healthy walk."

"Just what I need," said Roy, smiling ingratiatingly. "Ready for another drink, Aggie?"

TWO

✝

SIR Charles Fraith sat at his desk in his study and looked again at the letter from the Dembley Walkers. It was signed by a Ms. Jessica Tartinck and was militant, to say the least. "You aristocrats think you own the countryside," went one sentence. "But we do," murmured Sir Charles. "I own this land, anyway." He looked at it again. It claimed that there was an old right of way across his land. He spread out the maps of his property. There was a thin dotted line marking the right of way. He had never even noticed it before. They could use it all right, but with one exception. At one point it went right through a field of oil-seed rape. These old rights of way had originally been paths to the school or the church or work, as far back as the Middle Ages. They were not really intended for suburbanites to clump across in serious boots.

Sir Charles was a baronet who lived in a large Victorian mansion which commanded one thousand acres of good arable land. Although in his mid-thirties, he was still unmarried. He was a small neat man with fine fair hair and a mild, sensitive face. In him occasionally warred three characters. There was the bluff squire type, rather hearty, given to rather obvious jokes and puns; then there was the clever intellectual who never talked about his first in history from Cambridge; and then there was the withdrawn character who really trusted no one and did not like anyone to get too close to him.

He lived with a faded aunt, his late mother's sister, a Mrs. Tassy who, although absent-minded, acted as hostess for him at house parties and saw to little else. The running of the household fell on the shoulders of his late father's butler, Gustav. Gustav still styled himself "butler," but in these days of dwindling servants, Gustav was really a sort of houseman, doing light cooking when required, ordering in the groceries and wine, and helping out sometimes in the garden, or with the housework if one of the cleaners who came in from the village fell ill. He was no old retainer but was in his early fifties and kept his country of origin a well-guarded secret. He had a clever, mobile face, a male dancer's figure, and small black eyes.

He came into the room quietly and began to make up the fire, for the day had turned chilly. Sir Charles held out the letter. "What do you think of this, Gustav?"

Gustav took out a pair of spectacles and scanned the letter. "Screw the silly bitch," he said.

"Probably not screwable, Gustav. Can't offend them or they'll put in a complaint under the 1980 Highways Act, and you know what a trouble that will cause. Best to send back the soft answer, hey? Tell you what, I'll tell them this time to walk *round* the edge of that field and invite them for tea."

"Got more to do with my time than serve tea to a

bunch of Commie-bastards," said Gustav.

"You'll do as you're told," said Sir Charles mildly.

He rolled up the maps and proceeded to write a polite letter to Ms. Jessica Tartinck.

The Carsely Ramblers gathered outside Harvey's, the post office/general stores on Sunday.

At first Agatha had only eyes for James. "Back again," he said mildly.

"Thank you for looking after my garden," said Agatha, suddenly wishing Roy weren't glued to her side.

"Not at all." He turned away and addressed the small group. There was Mrs. Mason, the chairwoman of the Carsely Ladies Society; Miss Simms, the society's secretary; Mrs. Bloxby, the vicar's wife; Mr. and Mrs. Harvey from the stores; Jack Page, a local farmer, and two of his teen-age children; and, horror upon horrors, that elderly and constantly complaining couple, Mr. and Mrs. Boggle. Although the sun was shining, the day was unseasonably cold, and grey clouds were piling up in the west.

"Now, as it is so cold," said James, raising his voice, "we will walk up to Lord Pendlebury's estate by the back road. There is a pretty walk round the edge of the fields that we haven't been on yet. Nothing too strenuous. Are you sure you are up to this, Mr. and Mrs. Boggle?"

"Course," said Mrs. Boggle truculently. "Us'll probably do better than this young whipper-snapper here." She jerked a thumb at Roy.

James set off. Agatha wanted to run forward and walk with him but felt suddenly shy. He was as handsome as ever with his thick greying hair, tanned face, and blue eyes. She fell into step beside Mrs. Bloxby.

21

"Nice to see you back," said the vicar's wife. "It's been a dreary winter. Horrible weather. Nothing dramatic, just rain and more rain."

"You don't notice the changing seasons much in the City," said Agatha. "Just look at the weight I've put on! Taking taxis everywhere and eating expensive food."

"This is as good a way as any to take it off," said Mrs. Bloxby. "I really find it hard to have Christian thoughts about the Boggles."

"Is this the first time they have turned up?"

"Yes, and how they will stay the distance, I do not know."

"Don't walk so fast," shouted Mrs. Boggle, and they all slowed down to a crawl.

"They'll give up in a minute," said Mrs. Bloxby on a sigh, "and demand someone runs them home, and somehow I fear that someone is going to be me. Did you enjoy your stay in London?"

"Aggie was a whiz," put in Roy eagerly. "Best PR ever."

"And according to you, the most unpopular one ever," said Agatha waspishly.

"Just my joke, sweetie. You always take things too seriously."

"I have always wondered," commented Mrs. Bloxby, "why it is when someone says something cruel or offensive, they immediately try to cover it up by saying, 'It was only a joke. Can't you take a joke?' There was a woman, a visitor to the vicarage, the other day, who said, 'Don't you just look like a typical vicar's wife!' I said crossly I did not think I looked like a typical anything and she said, 'Can't you take a joke?' But she said it so nastily, you know, obviously implying that I looked mild, correct, prim, and faded. I could have struck her. Oh, here we go!"

Mrs. Boggle's voice was raised in complaint. "Me heart! Me heart! Take me home before I die."

"I'd better go," said Mrs. Bloxby regretfully.

To Agatha's dismay, James swung around. "No, you stay. I'll get my car. Go ahead. I'll come back and catch up with you." He set off back down the hill with long athletic strides. They waited while Mrs. Boggle panted and gasped and her husband muttered it was all their fault for keeping up such a cracking pace, no consideration for the elderly, and young people these days were downright selfish, ignoring the fact that Roy was the only member of the party, apart from Miss Simms, who could be considered young.

After James had driven up and collected the Boggles, the rest of them walked on. A chill wind from the north rustled the young leaves of the trees over their heads. Everything was very fresh and green. They turned off onto the back road which ran along the edge of Lord Pendlebury's estate. Fields of oil-seed rape spread out on either side, virulent yellow, Provençal yellow.

"Not allergic to rape, are we, Mrs. Raisin?" called out Mrs. Mason.

"Chance would be a fine thing," Roy giggled. "At her age, our Aggie takes anything she can get."

"Shut your face," exclaimed Agatha wrathfully.

"Just my joke," said Roy, avoiding Mrs. Bloxby's clear gaze.

Oh, this is not what I expected, thought Agatha. I thought I could sink back into Carsely like lying back in a warm bath. I wish Roy hadn't come. He seems to have brought that part of myself I don't like with him from

London. She cast a covert glance at him. His thin white face was pinched with cold. Why had he come? At first she had naïvely thought he had regretted his remarks, but now she was not so sure. Roy moved away to speak to Miss Simms.

"So are your PR days really over?" The vicar's wife looked inquiringly at Agatha. "Oh, I hope so." Agatha, looking out across the golden fields, felt quite weak and tearful again. Was this the menopause at last? Was she tired? "The last account was the pits, Pop singer called Jeff Loon. I had to sweet-talk some pill from the *Daily Bugle*."

"Would that be Ross Andrews?"

"Why, yes!"

"We take the *Daily Bugle*. There was a big spread about Jeff Loon, highly complimentary, on the entertainments page. Was that your doing?"

"As a matter of fact, it was." Agatha stared at Roy. Suddenly she was sure she knew what had happened. She herself had not even bothered buying a copy of the *Daily Bugle*. But that spread would make a tremendous impact in the PR world. She knew for the first time how much Pedmans would want her back. Wilson must have sent Roy down, and so the nasty little creep had oiled his way onto the train, babbling, "Don't worry. I'll get her back."

The party started to climb over a stile onto a path which ran alongside a field. It was a muddy path. Agatha was wearing flat shoes, fine for walking in London, but not really suitable for the country. Roy was wearing loafers and thin socks. Miss Simms was wearing a pair of Dr. Martens and Agatha reflected it was the first time she had seen Carsely's unmarried mother wearing anything other than spindly high heels. Roy squelched into a muddy puddle and let out a wail of dismay.

He turned back and joined Agatha. "Let's jack this in." But Agatha, who had been turning round from time to time to see if James was coming back, saw his tall figure climbing over the stile, and said curtly, "Don't whine. The exercise is good for you." Then she, too, stepped in a puddle, but now that James was catching up with the group, she was determined not to notice it.

"This land," said James, "used to belong to the church. Then it was part of the Hurford estate. Lord Hurford lost his money gambling in the twenties and Pendlebury bought it from him. He had a place in Yorkshire but didn't like the climate. That was the present Lord Pendlebury's father. Now that little blue flower just at your feet, Mrs. Mason, is . . ." He looked around. "Can anyone tell me?"

"Like being back in bloody school," muttered Roy.

"Speedwell," said Mrs. Bloxby.

"Very good," said James with such warmth and approval in his voice that Agatha decided to buy a book on wild flowers and plants and study it before the next ramble. She had expected a gentle tour around the fields and then back home, but the indefatigable walkers ploughed ahead through woods and fields until, with a feeling of relief, Agatha saw the spire of the church and knew they were circling back home and were nearly at Carsely.

James finally joined Agatha. "So now you are back with us, can we expect any more murders?"

"Oh, I shouldn't think so," said Agatha, although guiltily wishing that someone in the village would bump someone off so that she and James could go detecting again.

James looked thoughtfully down at Agatha. There was something rather sad and lost at the back of her eyes. He wanted the old truculent and confident Agatha back. "Why don't I call for you in a hour," he said suddenly, "and we'll have a drink together at the Red Lion?"

"I would love that," said Agatha.

"Bring your friend, of course."

"He will be *much* too tired," retorted Agatha. Roy had only come down because Wilson had told him to. He was not going to spoil her evening.

And so a sulky Roy was told to watch television until she came home.

Agatha searched feverishly through her wardrobe for something attractive that would not look too overdressed. Everything felt tight. She tried on dresses and skirts and blouses, settling for a comfortable old tweed skirt and sweater at the very last minute. Life was once more full of excitement and colour. She was home.

Bugger London!

Deborah Camden trudged up the long drive which led to Sir Charles Fraith's mansion. Jessica had ordered her to walk over the route and check it out, but Deborah did not want to find herself facing some angry landowner or keeper all on her own and had decided it would be less frightening to call at the house first and explain her presence. To people who love architectural gems, Barfield House might appear a disappointment. It was not even Victorian Gothic. It was a large building built in the fake medieval style, vaguely William Morris, with mullioned windows on which the sun sparkled and winked.

The door was massive and studded. Deborah looked timidly around to see if there was perhaps not a smaller and less intimidating door but could not see anything. There was an electric bell on the wall at the side. She rang it and waited.

The door was opened by a man in a black suit, white shirt, and plain silk tie. He had grizzled hair, small black eyes, and a long mouth. He studied her impassively, and yet Deborah was suddenly sharply aware of the cheapness of everything she was wearing.

"Yes?" he demanded.

"Sir Charles Fraith?"

"Who wants him?"

"I represent the Dembley Walkers." A thin line of sweat was forming on Deborah's upper lip.

A voice called out, "Who is it, Gustav?"

The man turned and said evenly. "A person from the Dembley Walkers, sir."

Gustav drew back and his place was taken by Sir Charles. He blinked at Deborah and said. "You're a girl. I thought it might be one of those big beefy chaps with big beefy boots. Come in."

Deborah walked into a vast oak-panelled hall. A moose head glared down at her from high up near the "boat" ceiling, wooden and arched like those in old churches. Sir Charles led the way into a drawing-room, with Chippendale chairs upholstered in red and cream, a large fire, oak-panelled walls like the hall, and long mullioned windows looking out over the park, where deer flitted through the trees.

"Tea," said Sir Charles to the hovering Gustav. Gustav moved noiselessly forward, picked a log out of a basket beside the fire and hurled it into the flames with unnecessary force before going out of the room.

27

"Now, Miss . . . ?"

Deborah held out a thin hand. "Deborah Camden. Pleased ter meet you."

"And very pleased to meet you. Sit down. Sit down. I received a letter from a Mizz Tartinck. I have just sent off a reply. Part of the right of way runs straight through one of my fields. There is, however, quite a pretty walk round the edge of that field. If you would be content with that, I would be glad to supply you all with tea."

"Oh, you are awfully kind," said Deborah. She was beginning to relax. Sir Charles looked so mild and inoffensive, and Jessica could not turn down such a generous invitation.

Sir Charles smiled at her. He thought she was a decent sort of girl. She had thick, pale, fair hair, permed into curls and waves in a rather old-fashioned style. Her face was very white, almost anaemic, and she wore no make-up. She had white lashes and pale-blue eyes. Her thin figure, encased in a cheap little white nylon blouse, acrylic skirt, and droopy wool cardigan, was thin and flat-chested. She had very long legs under the short skirt, with rather knobby knees which Sir Charles decided he found rather exciting.

"This Mizz Tartinck sounds a formidable sort of lady," said Sir Charles.

"Oh, she's a darling, really," said Deborah, "and awfully well educated. She's a schoolteacher like me and should really be teaching somewhere better than Dembley Comprehensive."

Wouldn't be able to rule the roost at a more distinguished school, thought Sir Charles, but he said aloud, "Well, if the rest of the Dembley Walkers are like you, Deborah, then it should be quite a jolly day."

"They get a bit hot under the collar about landowners," volunteered Deborah.

"Why?"

"Well . . . er . . . they feel the countryside ought to belong to everyone."

"But if, say, I did not own and run this estate, what would happen to it? People can't afford places like this these days. I mean, it might be sold off in lots to a builder, and bang! goes another slab of countryside. Absolutely shiters, that. I don't want to appear hard. Not a hard man, Deborah. Soft as butter. But I notice that there are rights of way sometimes through council estates and things but you lot don't demand the right to march through *their* gardens, now do you?"

"I suppose not. But don't you think it is an unfair society where someone like you should have so much and other people so little?"

"No, as a matter of fact."

"Oh."

The door opened and Gustav came in carrying a tray heavy with tea-things. "What's this, Gustav, my man?" demanded Sir Charles. "No cakes or biscuits?"

"I'll get them," said Gustav.

The tray was set on a low table in front of the fire between Deborah and Sir Charles.

"Shall I be mother?" asked Deborah.

Gustav rolled his eyes and muttered audibly, "Saints preserve us," before exiting again.

Deborah blushed painfully. "What did I say wrong? I just meant I would pour the tea."

"So you did, and so you shall. Don't pay any attention to Gustav. He's potty."

Gustav came back in carrying a plate with cakes. As his return was so quick, Deborah guessed that he had expected Sir Charles to demand cakes and had left the plate somewhere outside the door. Gustav shook out a napkin and placed it on Deborah's lap, contempt in every line of his expressive body.

She found her hands were beginning to tremble and said, in almost a whisper, "Perhaps Gustav should serve."

"See to it, Gustav."

Deborah murmured that, yes, she took milk and sugar, and heaved a sigh of relief when Gustav left the room again.

"So tell me about yourself," said Sir Charles. "What do you teach?"

"Physics."

"How clever of you."

"Not really clever," said Deborah. "And I hardly ever get a bright pupil. But this is my second teaching job. Maybe I'll move on next year."

"Any of the pupils give you a hard time?"

"Oo, yes. There was this nasty boy, Elvis Black. Ever so horrible. Always jeering and breaking things. But Jessica went round and had a word with his parents. I don't know what she said, but he's been quiet as a lamb ever since."

Sir Charles was beginning to regret his invitation to the Dembley Walkers to take tea with him. He was rapidly coming to the conclusion that Jessica was every bit as horrible as she sounded in her letter. But he liked Deborah. He liked her inoffensive quiet manner, he liked her pale, bleached look. He particularly liked those knees. The more she talked about her school life, the more she relaxed, and only Gustav coming back in to throw yet another unnecessary log on the fire made her look at her watch and say that she had better be getting back.

"I'll run you home," said Sir Charles.

"No, it's all right," said Deborah, conscious of Gustav's black eyes on her. "I left my little car down at the lodge-gates. I like walking, really."

Sir Charles stood up at the same time as Deborah. "Give me your phone number," he said. "We must do this again." Deborah fumbled in her bag and found a piece of paper and a pen. She scribbled down her phone number.

"I will show miss out," said Gustav.

Gustav held open the massive front door for Deborah. She ducked her head as she passed him, but he said suddenly, "Don't get any ideas about Sir Charles. He isn't for the likes of you. So keep your little hands in your pockets and your feet off this estate."

Deborah was too intimidated to reply. She walked off down the drive, her face flaming. The only thought that gave her any comfort was that Jessica would soon put Gustav in his place.

The Dembley Walkers crowded into the small classroom which they used for their meetings that evening. Jessica looked flushed and excited. She stood up and read out Sir Charles's letter in a jeering voice. "As if we're going to be bribed with offers of tea," she finished. She looked at Deborah. "Did you check out the route this afternoon?"

Deborah stood up. "Not exactly," she said. "I called at the house first and Sir Charles gave me tea and he was awfully nice. I mean, he's looking forward to seeing us, Jessica."

"So the great man gives you tea and you roll over and play dead," sneered Jessica. "Honestly, Deborah, what a wet you are. I should have gone myself."

Jeffrey Benson, Jessica's lover, unexpectedly rose to Deborah's defence. "Sounds a nice fellow to me. That was a decent letter, Jessica. I don't know about the rest of you, but I thought we were all supposed to be walking for enjoyment."

Terry Brice, the waiter, nudged his friend, Peter Hatfield, in the ribs and sniggered, "Nice to be served tea by someone else for a change."

Alice Dewhurst boomed out, "I am all for confronting landowners, Jessica, and no one intimidates me. But when the man has gone out of his way to write a nice letter and all we have to do is walk around the edge of one field, I don't see what the fuss is about."

"It's a matter of *principle*," said Jessica, thin eyebrows raised, still confident of beating them down. "Don't tell me you are all so thrilled at the idea of tea with one minor aristocrat that you are going to let him get away with this?"

"Well, ah, I cannae see anything wrong with the man," said Kelvin Hamilton. "We're a wee bittie mair democratic up in the Highlands, and—"

"Oh, spare us tales of Brigadoon," said Jessica. "We all know you come from Glasgow and probably some slum at that."

"You bitch!" shouted Kelvin. "Go yoursel'. I'm sick o' you." He stormed out. There was an uneasy silence.

Mary Trapp stood up on her large feet. "You know, Jessica," she said, "no one appointed you leaderene of this group or whatever. If you're determined to make trouble,

I'm not going." And to Jessica's dismay, there was a murmur of assent.

Jessica went into her favourite speech on equality and feminism, quotes from Marx and Simone de Beauvoir. Her eyes flashed. She looked magnificent, but she was heard out in a stony silence.

"All right," she finished, glaring around at them. "I'm going. And I'm going to walk right across that field!"

Agatha Raisin waved goodbye to Roy with a feeling of relief, glad that she had ordered him a taxi and that she did not have to drive him to the station. She was sick of the sight of him. She had been enjoying a pleasant chat with James on the Sunday evening and Roy had sidled into the pub, smiling ingratiatingly all round and then had monopolized her, telling her how much Pedmans wanted her back while James's attention had been claimed by other villagers. Agatha fervently hoped she would never see him again.

She felt quite stiff and sore after her ramble but was convinced that her skirt was a tiny bit loose around the waist. She resolved to diet, or rather, instead of going on a formal diet, to eat fewer calories.

Then, to get closer to James again—although she would not even admit to herself that that was her motive— she decided to get really involved with the Carsely Ramblers. They needed to be organized, have meetings, stick-up posters announcing their forthcoming rambles, and so on. There was no need for them to confine their walks to around the village. They could use their cars to go farther afield, have a meeting-point at some pleasant country pub, and start walking from there.

Agatha drove down to the second-hand bookshop in Moreton and found an old book on various rights of way. Then, fired with enthusiasm, she returned to the village and knocked boldly on James's door.

"Oh, Agatha," was the unwelcoming greeting, "I was just getting a good run on my book. But come in."

Agatha felt she should really say something like, "Oh, well, in that case, I'll come back later," but she had been away so long and James had been writing that wretched piece of military history for so long that she was sure a short interruption would not matter.

"I had some ideas for the Carsely Ramblers," said Agatha eagerly as he stood back to let her in.

"Such as?" he asked, switching off his word processor. "Coffee?"

"Yes, please." She followed him into the kitchen.

"I thought," said Agatha, "that we might get a bit more organized. You know, maybe take our cars and go somewhere farther afield and start from there."

"I suppose we could do that," he said on a sigh. "As a matter of fact, Agatha, I was thinking of dropping the whole thing."

"Why?"

"I'm not really the organizing type."

"I can do all that for you. All you have to do is show up."

"Do you take milk and sugar?"

"Black, no sugar," said Agatha, thinking he might at least have remembered how she liked her coffee. They carried their mugs through to the book-lined living-room. She lit a cigarette and looked round for an ashtray. He rose and went back to the kitchen and returned with an old saucer which he put down next to her. Why was it non-smokers always made one feel so guilty? thought Agatha. Hardly anyone had an ashtray in the house any more.

The smoke from her cigarette rose to the beamed ceiling and hung there. James's eyes followed it as if measuring pollution.

"So what had you in mind?" asked James. A car slowed down in the lane outside. He looked hopefully towards the window, as if longing for some interruption.

"Like I said, we could go farther away for our rambles and maybe I could work out some posters and put one up in Harvey's and one on the church notice-board. We get a few tourists and they might like to come along. Then I thought we should have membership cards and charge a fee."

"I don't know about a fee," said James. "I mean, what would the fee be for? Landowners don't charge the public for using rights of way. That," he added pedantically, "is why they are called rights of way."

"A fee would pay for membership cards. People like having membership cards."

"I don't. Look, Agatha, I really should get on. Why don't you go ahead and see what you can organize and then let me know about it?"

Agatha looked pointedly down into her coffee-cup as if indicating that she had had hardly time to drink any, but then she put the cup down and made her way to the door. James walked after her, switching on the word processor again on the way.

Well, that's that, thought Agatha gloomily, letting herself into her own cottage. Sod ramblers. A car drew up behind her and she turned round to see Detective Sergeant Bill Wong smiling at her from the driving seat.

"Welcome back," he cried, getting out, his features creased in a smile.

"Come in," cried Agatha. "We'll have coffee and you can tell me all about crime. I've just been to James's but got turfed out after about two minutes."

"Oh, is that still going on?"

"Is what still going on?"

"Your deathless love for James Lacey."

"Don't be silly. I used to have a little crush on him, but that's long gone." Agatha walked into the kitchen and put on the kettle. "We have a rambling group in Carsely now. James was running it. All I suggested was that it could do with a bit more organization."

"Not one of those militant groups, Agatha."

"No, no. Quiet little walks, but maybe better publicized and with membership cards and things like that."

"I'm sure you'll do it. So how was London?"

"Dire."

"No fun being back in harness?"

"None at all. Glad to be home. The reason I got so interested in the rambling thing is I badly need to lose weight."

"Don't we all," said Bill mournfully, looking down at his own chubby figure.

"So how's crime?"

"Quiet since you left. Usual wife beatings, drunks on a Saturday night, burglary, stolen cars, and general mayhem. A few murders but nothing exotic." He looked at her with affection. "You're longing to play detective again, Agatha. Don't.

"Take my advice and stick to rambling. Nice quiet pursuit. Rambling never leads to murder!"

THREE

✝

JESSICA sat moodily on the end of the bed on Monday evening and said to her lover, Jeffrey Benson, who was propped up against the pillows, "I don't know what came over that little twit, Deborah. Or the rest of you, for that matter."

Jeffrey scratched his hairy chest. "Come on, Jessica. I'm all for fighting nasty landowners, but when one of the breed is civil enough to send us a decent letter and issue an invitation to tea, then I'm prepared to meet him half-way. And if you plan on clumping over his precious field, then you can bloody well go alone."

"I didn't think you would let me down like this, after all we've been to each other."

"Don't use emotional blackmail on me, Jessica. You were the one who said that all we had going for each other was sex. The trouble with you feminists is that your idea of equality is to adopt the nastier characteristics of the men you despise. Maybe I should take up with Deborah. She's showing some good old-fashioned female characteristics."

An ugly light came into Jessica's eyes. "You'd better watch your mouth, Jeffrey *dear*. I mean, don't you think MI5 might be interested in that couple of Irishmen you gave house room to two years ago?"

A wary look shone in his eyes. "How'd you know about that? You weren't here."

"You got blind drunk after Alice's party and bragged about it. I mean, that would be around the time that IRA bomb went off in the High Street and killed a child."

"It was nothing to do with them. They were just friends of friends who wanted a bed. They only stayed two nights."

"Oh, but in your cups you mumbled away about striking a blow for the freedom of Ireland." She threw her head back and laughed, an irritatingly stagy laugh.

He plunged across the bed and seized her by the throat. He was a powerful man. One brown eye which had a slight cast gave him a sinister look when he was angry. "You dare to tell *anyone* about those Irishmen and I'll kill you. We're finished. Get your stuff and get out, by the morning."

Jessica struck at his hands. Her eyes flashed. "I'm not frightened of you." He sat back on the bed on his heels, a powerful naked figure.

"Oh, but you should be, Jessica. You should be."

That was Monday evening.

"It's good of you to put me up," said Jessica, looking around Deborah's small flat. "I don't know what came over Jeffrey. But that's men for you."

"Well, he has a point," said Deborah. "Why must you insist on going through with it?"

"Because Sir Charles stands for everything we are

against. Privilege, unfair wealth, keeping people from enjoying the countryside. Oh, let's not argue." She smiled slowly down into Deborah's eyes. "Let's go to bed. I feel like an early night."

"All right," sighed Deborah. "I'll make us some coffee first. Put your stuff in the bedroom."

As Jessica walked through to the bedroom, the phone rang. Deborah picked up the receiver. "Hello there," came the voice of Sir Charles Fraith. "Look, there's a showing of *Citizen Kane* at the Art Cinema tomorrow night. Feel like seeing it with me and having a bit of supper afterwards?"

"Love to," said Deborah, clutching the phone hard and marvelling that there was someone still left on the planet who hadn't seen *Citizen Kane*.

"Give me your address and I'll pick you up."

Deborah looked nervously towards the bedroom. "No, I'll meet you there. What time?"

"Begins at seven-thirty. Meet you outside at quarter past."

"Yes, thank you."

"See you then. 'Bye."

Deborah walked into the bedroom, a mulish look on her normally weak face. "I think I'll sleep on the sofa," she said to Jessica. "And I like my space. You can only stay here the one night."

Jessica looked at her, feeling a hot burst of rage. What had happened to all her acolytes? "Who was that on the phone?" she demanded.

"Just a friend," said Deborah. "I do have friends other than you, you know."

"I'll bet it was Jeffrey."

Deborah remained silent, with the set stubbornness of

the weak and frightened stamped on her face.

"So it *was* Jeffrey," said Jessica. "Well, before you get the hots for that oaf, just think what he would say if he knew you had sex with me that evening he was away at the teachers' conference in Birmingham."

"You wouldn't," shouted Deborah, not giving a damn what Jeffrey would think, but terrified that any such gossip would get around and might reach the ears of Sir Charles, her mind so distorted by fear that she did not pause to think it highly unlikely any part of her world would cross that of Sir Charles Fraith.

"Oh, I would, I would."

"Get out in the morning!" screamed Deborah, beside herself with fear and hatred. "I never want to see you again."

That was Tuesday.

Happy and quite drunk, Kelvin Hamilton lay in bed and watched Jessica strip. He had hardly been able to believe his luck when she had arrived on his doorstep with her two suitcases, claiming to have always fancied him. Past insults were forgotten. He was not surprised that she did not wear a bra and had breasts that were quite magnificent. This, he thought, was going to be a night to remember. When she removed her jeans and he saw she was wearing men's Y-fronts, he felt a sudden sharp diminution of lust.

She climbed into bed and he proceeded to try to make love to her, but nothing happened. After he seemed to have been thrashing around on top of her for some time, Jessica said in a disgusted voice, "Oh, for heaven's sake, Kelvin, give up. You've got distiller's droop. Go to sleep." The contempt in her voice sobered him. Soon she was gently snoring. He lay with the tears rolling down his cheeks. He thought he would die of sheer humiliation. He wanted her dead. He woke her up and began to shout.

That was Wednesday night.

Jessica was determined to find free lodgings. She called at the Copper Kettle, but Peter and Terry squeaked nervously like bats and backed away from her. "Haven't an inch to spare, sweetie," said Terry. "Must rush. Lots of customers." So Jessica went round to Alice Dewhurst's, to the flat she shared with Gemma Queen.

"I'm all for helping one of the sisterhood," boomed Alice, "but as you can see, we really haven't room for anyone else. Have you tried the Y?"

And so Jessica moved in with Mary Trapp, whom she secretly despised and only found comfort in the fact that Mary slavishly adored her. Mary even said she would go with her on the walk across that field of Sir Charles Fraith's on Saturday.

But on the Friday, Mary complained of stomach pains. Then she disappeared to the bathroom, from which sickening retching noises could soon be heard.

"It's your own fault," said Jessica unsympathetically. "You will buy junk from the health shops and overeat, thinking it's all right because it comes from a health shop. Honestly, you are a pill."

"Leave me alone," said Mary.

"At least you should be fit enough to come with me tomorrow," said Jessica.

Mary hunched a shoulder. "I won't."

So on Saturday, wearing a large pair of studded boots, a short denim skirt and sleeveless blouse, and with a militant gleam in her eye, Jessica Tartinck set out alone.

On the following Monday, Jeffrey approached Deborah in the staff-room. "How's Jessica getting on?"

"I don't know," said Deborah. "I haven't seen her. I believe she moved in with Mary."

"I'm meeting the others for lunch in the Grapes," said Jeffrey, meaning the ramblers. "We'll ask her then."

But when they were all settled over their beer and sandwiches in the Grapes, it was to learn from Mary that Jessica had set out on her walk across Sir Charles's estate and had not returned.

"He probably sent her off with a flea in her ear and she blames all of us," commented Jeffrey. "You know she likes to sulk."

"She's a bitch," said Kelvin moodily.

"That's not true!" Mary looked outraged. "What's happened to all of you? You should be ashamed of yourselves."

"Why didn't you go with her, Mary?" asked Alice.

"I was too ill," said Mary. "Food poisoning."

"I'm a teensy bit worried." Peter looked around the group with wide eyes. "The poor thing came to the Copper Kettle looking for a bed from us. Did you throw her out, Jeffrey?"

"Yes," he said curtly. "What happened with you, Deborah? Didn't she try you?"

"I've got a small flat, as you know, and only one bed," said Deborah. "I could only give her one night's lodgings."

"I said we should have put her up," whispered Gemma.

Alice's eyes flashed with jealousy. "Now, we're not going to have a row about that again."

"So what should I do?" asked Mary. "Call the police?"

"We don't want to have anything to do with the filth," said Jeffrey, and there was a general murmur of agreement. "I'll ask Jones if he's heard anything from her." Mrs. Jones was the head-teacher.

"I've already done that," said Deborah. "I asked this morning. She hasn't phoned in sick or anything."

"Then maybe you'd better ask your friend, Sir Charles, if he saw her on Saturday," suggested Jeffrey, looking at Deborah.

"No friend of mine," muttered Deborah. She had not told the others of her date with Sir Charles. She had enjoyed her evening, although, in her case, seeing *Citizen Kane* for the umpteenth time and then being entertained to supper in a Burger King had not seemed like an upper-class evening out. But Sir Charles had been easy company, although he had not suggested seeing her again. She longed to phone him. Now, surely, she had an excuse to do so.

"I could phone him up," she offered.

"Knowing Jessica," tittered Peter," she could already be shacked up with him."

"I'll phone," said Deborah.

She went over to the public phone in the corner, Gustav answered the phone. She breathlessly asked for Sir Charles. "Sir Charles is not at home," said Gustav.

"Oh, I wondered if you had seen anything of my friend, Miss Jessica Tartinck?"

"No."

And then, somewhere in the regions of the house behind Gustav, Deborah distinctly heard Sir Charles calling, "Who is it, Gustav?"

"No one," called back Gustav and put the phone down.

Deborah stared at the receiver in baffled fury. Then she slowly replaced it. Pride stopped her from telling the others she had been snubbed by a servant.

"No, he hasn't heard anything," she said.

Jeffrey looked at her in surprise. "But didn't one of his keepers or gardeners see her?"

"No," said Deborah, head bent.

"Now what do we do?" demanded Alice.

"We're not in the pages of a Gothic romance," said Jeffrey. "I mean, if you're thinking she's in the deepest dungeon of Barfield House in chains, forget it."

"It may have nothing to do with Sir Charles," said Gemma. "All sorts of awful things happen to women these days."

"Wimmin like Jessica mug folks, they don't get mugged themselves," said Kelvin.

It was at last agreed to leave the matter for another couple of days. A few more drinks and they all began to feel confident that Jessica was staying away to get even with them for having stood up to her.

But two more days passed, and the Dembley Walkers met in the school.

No Jessica. It was Jeffrey who addressed the group. "I think we should all get together after work tomorrow and go out there and see if we can see any sign of her."

"No need for that," said Mary Trapp. "I'm convinced

she is staying away to punish and frighten us."

"An' I say, whit do we pay taxes for?" demanded Kelvin truculently. "Call the cops."

"No," retorted Jeffrey fiercely. "Let's see what we can do ourselves first."

It was a clear warm evening when they all met up again. Ill-assorted as they were, Jeffrey could not help thinking how relaxed and happy they all were without Jessica around. She had dominated them so much. He mentally pulled himself up. He was already thinking of her in the past tense. They marched out of Dembley in the golden evening. When they reached Sir Charles's estate, Jeffrey unfurled a large ordnance survey map of the Pathfinder series and with one grubby fingernail outlined the route.

A silence fell on the group. Without the militant Jessica heading them, none could get away from an uneasy feeling of trespass. The evening was very still and quiet. They carefully shut farm gates behind them. Jessica would have left them open. Soon they reached the field of oil-seed rape blazing golden in the westering sunlight.

"Look!" said Jeffrey, stopping at the edge of the field. Jessica, they assumed it must have been Jessica, had certainly marched right into the field, trampling and stamping down the flowers.

"She must have *jumped* her way along to do this damage," said Alice, quite awed.

They fell into single file, Jeffrey at the head, and followed the track. Over the trees at the far end of the field rose the bulk of Barfield House.

"The track stops here," said Jeffrey. "Was she burying something?"

45

They all gathered around and looked down at the mound of earth and torn yellow flowers.

Kelvin edged forward and scraped at the earth with one large foot. A little cascade of loose earth fell from the mound and there, sticking out, was a booted foot and a white leg, a white hairy leg. Jessica never shaved her legs.

"Oh, God," shrieked Alice. She knelt down and scrabbled at the earth with her fingers. Gradually Jessica's body was exposed. Her earth-soiled face stared sightlessly up to the calm evening sky.

Deborah turned away and was violently sick, Gemma began to weep and Mary Trapp fainted, falling over the dead body in a grotesque embrace.

Kelvin pulled her away. "We've done enough. Get the police. Don't you daft pillocks see? Someone's murdered her!"

It was quickly discovered, once Jessica's body had been turned over, that someone had struck her a vicious blow on the back of the head with a spade, striking down with the edge, and then had made an ineffectual attempt to bury her. Bill Wong, waiting patiently by the tent which now covered Jessica's body for one of his superiors to give him instructions, had a fleeting thought that it was odd that Agatha should return from London to take up rambling and now here was a rambling murder. The lights placed on the field round the tent blazed into the darkness. An owl hooted from the trees. A rising wind rustled the oil-seed-rape blossoms, bleached white by the lights.

Detective Chief Inspector Wilkes came up to him. "They're all at the house, are they?"

Bill nodded.

"We'd better start questioning them. We've learned all we can at the moment. She was struck violently from behind."

"Must have been a pretty powerful man."

"No, a woman could have done it. One good swing. It was a heavy spade."

"So who would have a spade to hand?"

"That's what we've got to find out. Too early for fingerprints yet. And it's been raining since the murder, if she set out last Saturday, as she threatened to do."

"Think Sir Charles lost his rag and biffed her?".

"We'll get a better idea of what sort of man he is after we speak to him. I hear the bane of your life is back in Carsely."

"My friend Agatha?" Bill grinned. "I wonder what she'll make of this."

Wilkes shuddered. "Don't even tell her."

Gustav greeted them at the door. "I have put the persons you wish to question in the ballroom."

"We would like a word with Sir Charles first, if we may?"

Gustav inclined his head. "Come this way." His formal manner suddenly dropped. "And don't take all night over it. He looked over their shoulders. "What is it, Parsons?"

The policeman turned round. A tall thin man with a broken shotgun in the crook of his arm stood there.

"I have shut the gates, Gustav," said Parsons. "But the press are trying to get to the house."

"Then shoot them," said Gustav patiently. "This way, gentlemen." He held open the door of Sir Charles's study.

Wilkes hesitated a moment, obviously wondering if that order to shoot the press was to be taken seriously, and then decided it wasn't.

He introduced himself and Bill Wong.

Sir Charles sat behind a large leather-topped desk. He folded his hands neatly on top of it and surveyed them with bright interest.

"Now, Sir Charles," said Wilkes. "Just a few questions. The dead body in your field is that of a member of a rambling group called the Dembley Walkers. We believe she was killed last Saturday, possibly around the middle of the afternoon. That was the time she intended to be walking across your land. Did you see her?"

"No."

"Where were you last Saturday?"

"In London. I have a flat in Westminster."

"Address?"

He gave it to them.

"Did anyone see you?"

"Gustav drove me up and my aunt, Mrs. Tassy, came with us."

"We will be having a word with both Gustav and Mrs. Tassy."

"You can speak to Gustav for as long as you like. But must you speak to my aunt? She is lying down at the moment. All this has been a great shock to her."

"Perhaps tomorrow. But we must speak to her. Tell us what you know of the Dembley Walkers."

"Not much," said Sir Charles. "Here's a letter Miss Tartinck wrote to me and here's a copy of the letter I sent in return."

They studied both. Wilkes said, "So with such a

charming invitation, why was Miss Tartinck alone, do you think?"

"Oh, I can tell you that. I took one of the girls from the ramblers out to the picture house. *Citizen Kane.* Jolly good film. Have you seen it?"

"Many times," said Wilkes.

"Anyway, she said that the rest didn't like this Jessica's militant attitude and told her to go by herself."

"So you knew she was coming?"

"Yes, but I had friends to see in London and so I decided to make myself scarce."

"The name of these friends."

"The Hasseltons. But I didn't get around to seeing them. It was a wet day and I decided to stay in my flat and watch television."

"So you really have no witness to the fact that your were in London?"

"But I told you, my aunt and Gustav."

"We would have liked a witness less close to you."

"Meaning they would lie for me? That's a bit naughty."

"We'll speak to you again, if we may, Sir Charles," said Wilkes, getting to his feet.

"Must you? Don't be all night, will you?"

"Where would the murderer have found that spade?"

"I don't really know. I suggest you talk to my land agent, Mr. Temple. He lives in Dembley." Sir Charles scribbled on a piece of paper. "That's his address and phone number."

Wilkes took it. "Where are these ramblers?"

"I think Gustav's put them in the ballroom."

"Why there?" asked Wilkes curiously.

"I suppose because we hardly ever use it."

Wilkes turned in the doorway. "Which one of the ramblers was it you took out?"

"Nice little thing called Deborah Camden."

Gustav was waiting outside the door. He led the way across the vast expanse of the hall, down a corridor at the end and threw open a door. The ballroom was oak-panelled like the rest of the house. In a little island of chairs, which had been unshrouded from their covers for the occasion, sat the ramblers. A great Waterford chandelier blazed overhead. In the musicians' gallery overlooking the ballroom sat one policeman, and another stood guard beside the door.

Wilkes turned to Gustav. "I would like to question them one at a time. Is there somewhere we could use?"

Gustav hesitated and then said, "Come with me, sir."

He opened a door next to the ballroom. "Used to leave cloaks here in the old days," he said. "Good enough?"

Wilkes looked round. There were a few hard chairs, a long mirror along one wall, and nothing else except a black and empty fireplace.

"I suppose this will do. Send Deborah Camden in first."

"I have to attend to Sir Charles," said Gustav. "Get her yourself."

"I used to dream that one day I would be rich," said Bill Wong after Gustav had left, "and have servants. A short experience of Gustav is enough to persuade me that robots would be preferable."

"May as well get started instead of discussing the servant problem. Get Deborah in."

When Deborah came in, Wilkes studied her closely. She was very pale. A shy, insignificant little thing, he thought, amazed that Sir Charles should even consider dating her.

"This is just an initial interview, Miss Camden," he said. "We will need you to call at the police station tomorrow, where we will take an official statement. What were you doing last Saturday afternoon?"

"I went shopping in Dembley."

"And would any of the shop assistants remember you?"

"I shouldn't think so. I was window-shopping. A teacher's pay doesn't go very far."

"How is it you know Sir Charles?"

"I was sent out to check the right of way but I didn't want to be accused of trespass, so I called at the house. Sir Charles gave me tea, took my phone number, and then asked me out."

"We'll return to Sir Charles in a moment. What do you know of Jessica Tartinck?"

Deborah's eyes filled with tears. "I wish I hadn't quarrelled with her," she said shakily.

"Was the quarrel about the right of way?"

Deborah nodded dumbly.

"It's a sad business, but try to compose yourself. Tell us what you know of Jessica's background."

In a faltering voice, Deborah outlined what she knew. She knew Jessica had been with the anti-nuclear women protesters on Greenham Common when it had been a missile base. She had been arrested on a couple of occasions for cutting the wire. She had been vague about what posts in teaching she had held before she came to Dembley. No, no, they hadn't been *close*. Jessica had been living with Jeffrey Benson but he had thrown her out.

"Why?"

"The same reason that the rest of us got angry with her. She liked finding out rights of way that quite often the landowner didn't even know he had, and then making trouble. It was exciting for a bit, but I suppose we were all getting a bit tired of her bossing us around," said Deborah. "I'm only speculating, of course. I wasn't there when Jessica had the row with Jeffrey."

Deborah visibly grew more at ease as the questioning continued. She said that although Jessica seemed to have annoyed them all in one way or another, she could not think of anyone actually hating Jessica enough to kill her. "But I think I know who did," she ended triumphantly.

"Who?" demanded Wilkes.

"Gustav, that servant. He's weird and I think he could be violent."

"We'll be checking on him. We expect to see you at the central police headquarters in Mircester tomorrow to make a statement, Miss Camden. See the policeman at the door of the ballroom before you leave and he will give you a time to call on us. And send in Jeffrey Benson."

Bill Wong studied Jeffrey when he entered. Something was tugging at the back of his mind. He felt the police had been interested in Jeffrey before. Jeffrey Benson was a big, powerful man with receding hair tied back in a pony-tail.

He was warned it was a preliminary interview and then asked about his relations with Jessica Tartinck.

"We were lovers," said Jeffrey. "I suppose you want the old-fashioned term."

Being well aware of what the new-fashioned description would be, Wilkes pressed on.

"We'd like you to begin at the beginning and tell us

how it came about that Miss Tartinck went out walking along the old right of way on her own."

For one who did not like the police, Jeffrey appeared, surprisingly, an ideal witness. He described everything from the beginning, then Jessica's speech trying to rally them all, then how they had had a row, although he omitted any mention of Irishmen, simply saying he was tired of "bossy women." "There was no real affection between us," he said. "She wanted what I'd got and I gave it to her." Like Deborah, he had no alibi for the Saturday afternoon. He had done a few chores at home. Maybe he had gone to the Grapes. He couldn't really remember.

The next to be interviewed was Kelvin Hamilton. When asked if Jessica had applied to him for a place to stay, he said, "Of course not. I had no time for that lassie's bullying ways and she knew it." Kelvin thought furiously. He had not said anything to anyone of Jessica's visit. Had he? Then he thought with a sinking heart that the police might interview his neighbours, would *probably* interview his neighbours and might find out about the visit and the subsequent row. The walls between the flats were thin and Jessica had shouted a few choice insults at him on her road out. But he dare not tell them he had been lying. "I think you'll find it was Deborah Camden," he blustered.

"Why would that be?" asked Wilkes.

"Because she was so carried away wi' the idea o' being friendly wi' an aristo, och, you wouldnae think we was living in the twentieth century."

"And you think that would be enough motive to kill a woman for simply walking across a field?"

"It's the wee quiet ones you have tae watch."

They then took Kelvin through when he had first met

53

Jessica, what he knew of her, what he judged her relationship with Jeffrey to have been, and where he had been last Saturday, before letting him go, wiping the look of relief off his face by saying they would see him at police headquarters in Mircester the following day.

"Another one without an alibi for Saturday," said Wilkes.

The next was Alice Dewhurst. She wanted to be jointly interviewed with Gemma Queen and it took several minutes of argument to persuade her that they had to be seen separately.

Alice sat down sulkily after Gemma had been led away. "So," said Wilkes after Bill had taken down particulars of Alice's address, age, and job, "what can you tell us about Jessica Tartinck?"

She heaved her great bottom uneasily on the small hard chair. "I dunno. Seemed to have all the right ideas, but too pushy even for a dedicated feminist. I mean, it's the men you're supposed to push around, not the women."

Wilkes found this rather a mad piece of reasoning but he let it go.

Instead he said, "Did any of you know Jessica Tartinck before she came to Dembley?"

"No," said Alice. Something flickered at the back of her eyes. Bill Wong had an uneasy feeling she was lying.

"You will appreciate, Miss Dewhurst, that some of these questions may seem random, but it is important to establish what sort of person Miss Tartinck was. Miss Tartinck's family is in Milton Keynes, I believe she has a mother and sister living there, and they are being informed of her death. But she was killed here, and so we must try to find out why someone hated her enough to kill her."

"It's all very simple," said Alice in heavy patronizing tones. "Sir Charles or one of his minions on this estate lost their temper with her and struck her with a spade."

Wilkes reflected wryly that this reasoning seemed quite logical, as no one had made any attempts on Jessica's life before her solitary ramble, or none that they yet knew of. So they questioned Alice about Jessica, her interests, her friendships, and were left with a feeling that Alice had been jealous of Jessica and had not really liked her.

Alice said she had been at home with Gemma the previous Saturday. They had watched a video on television and had not gone out at all.

Gemma Queen, who was next, backed this alibi in a shy voice. She seemed to Wilkes to be typical of a certain type of unambitious shop-girl, the kind who should have been giggling about boy-friends with other shop-girls and not getting tied up with the tetchy and angry ramblers. Asked about Jessica, Gemma had nothing but praise and admiration for the dead woman.

"Did you share her militant views towards landowners?" asked Wilkes.

"Beg pardon?"

"Did you dislike landowners as much as Miss Tartinck?"

"You'll need to ask Alice."

"Miss Queen! Don't you have any views of your own?"

"I dunno. To tell the truth, I don't know half what they're talking about. But Jessica was all right. Real attractive. She took me to the ballet once." Gemma suddenly giggled. "Alice was furious."

Wilkes decided he wasn't going to get anything much out of Gemma that was useful. Besides, she would be interviewed again the following day. By that time they would know a lot more about the characters in the case.

Peter Hatfield and Terry Brice appeared refreshingly gossipy in comparison to the others. Both had been working on Saturday afternoon and appeared to be the only ones with cast-iron alibis. Although interviewed separately, their stories were much the same. Their motive in joining the walkers on their outings was because neither of them wanted to get "too fat." Yes, they usually took Saturday afternoon off, but this Saturday, when the restaurant was closed between three and seven, they had volunteered to stay on to set up the tables for the evening. Their stories were so alike that Wilkes was sure they had rehearsed them carefully while waiting in the ballroom. Although the one alibied the other, it did cross his mind that one of them could have left the restaurant, gone out to the estate in a car, murdered Jessica, and returned.

After them, he turned to Bill Wong, stretched and yawned and said, "Now, for Gustav."

But there was an interruption. A policeman who had been on guard outside the house came in and said, "Excuse me, sir, but one of the farm labourers is here. I think you should listen to him. His name is Noakes, Joe Noakes."

"Send him in."

A large, burly man with a bad-tempered-looking face came in. He said he was Joseph Noakes and worked on the home farm for Mr. Dyke, who ran it for the estate.

"And what have you got to tell us?"

"I seen Sir Charles and that dead woman."

Wilkes tensed.

"Go on. When?"

"Last Satterday, it were. Her was scraping and jumping her way across the rape field. Sir Charles met her."

"Where? Which part of the field? The middle, where the body was found?"

"No, t'war a bit towards the far side o' the field from the house."

"Could you hear what he was saying?"

"No, I war over in t'other field. But he was waving his fists at her. Then he turned away and walked back towards the house."

"And she was still alive?"

"Yerse," admitted Mr. Noakes with obvious reluctance.

"And then what happened?"

"I went away, didn't I, and saw nothing else."

"Wait outside," said Wilkes. "We'll be taking you down to the station."

When the door closed, he turned to Bill Wong.

"And we'll be taking Sir Charles as well. I think we've found our murderer."

FOUR

✝

AGATHA Raisin had just finished reading an account of the death of Jessica Tartinck in the local newspaper when her doorbell rang. Always hoping it might be James, she glanced quickly at her reflection in the hall mirror before opening the door.

Mrs. Mason, chairwoman of the Carsely Ladies Society, stood there. "Oh, Mrs. Raisin. May I come in a minute? I want to ask your advice."

"Of course. I was just about to have a cup of coffee." Agatha led the way through to the kitchen.

"So what can I do for you?" asked Agatha, pouring two mugs of coffee.

"It's this terrible murder. A relative of mine is involved."

Agatha's bearlike eyes gleamed with interest.

"My niece, Deborah Camden, is one of the ramblers," said Mrs. Mason. "She had heard through me of your detective abilities and begged me to speak to you. The fact is"—Mrs. Mason preened slightly—"that this Sir Charles Fraith is by way of being a friend of Deborah's."

"The landowner?"

"Yes, and Deborah says he has been arrested for the murder and that they've got the wrong person."

"Does she know the *right* person?"

"No, but she says Sir Charles is nice and kind and it can't be him."

"But there was nothing in the paper about an arrest. It simply said a man was helping police with their inquiries."

"That's Sir Charles. He hasn't been charged yet. But Deborah says it's only a matter of time. You see, he says he was up in London on the Saturday she was killed, but some farm labourer swears he saw Sir Charles in the field shouting at this Jessica and waving his arms."

"Oh dear, does she know why Sir Charles lied?"

"No. But she begged me to ask you for help."

"I would be delighted," said Agatha, speaking no more than the truth. She could hardly wait for Mrs. Mason to leave so that she could call on James and see if she could get him to join her in detecting adventures again.

But she asked, "What can you tell me about your niece?"

"Deborah is a schoolteacher at the Dembley Comprehensive. She is twenty-eight and not married. I haven't seen much of her because I quarrelled with her mother, Janice, my sister, a long time ago and we don't visit. Deborah always was a clever little thing but a bit mousy, which is probably why she isn't married."

"I think I should talk to her."

"She's teaching until four this afternoon. After that, I could take you over to Dembley."

"No, I don't want to be seen with her in Dembley," said Agatha.

"Why?"

"Well, perhaps I will be going undercover."

"Oh. Oh, well, I'll go over and fetch her and bring her to you. We'll be here about five."

"That would be splendid."

As soon as Mrs. Mason had left, Agatha darted upstairs and put on a new short-sleeved blouse of a soft leaf-green and then a pair of biscuit-coloured tailored slacks. Taking a deep breath to hold her stomach in, she made her way next door.

James opened the door. He frowned when he saw her. "What is it, Agatha? I'm very busy at the moment."

And Agatha, feeling hurt and rejected because he wasn't speaking any of the lines she had written for him in that short breathless time between Mrs. Mason's departure and Agatha's arrival at James's door, said gruffly, "Nothing. It can wait." And turned and walked away.

Screw him, she thought. Who needs him anyway? How dare he speak to me like that!

She found to her dismay that her interest in the case was waning fast. To counteract it, she drove down to the newsagent's in Moreton and bought all the papers and retreated to a dark corner of a tea-room, one of the few which still catered for smokers, and began to read all she could about the death of Jessica Tartinck.

Jessica, who had defied the others and said she would go on the walk on her own, had been found dead in the middle of one of the fields on Sir Charles Fraith's estate. She had been struck savagely on the back of the head with a spade. Jessica Tartinck had been a campaigner for all sorts of rights—anti-nuclear, save the whales, the environment in general, and now the rights of ramblers. A don from Oxford University described her as having a brilliant academic brain and absolutely no common sense whatsoever. She had taught at a girls' school and had brought the pupils out on strike. Although her family were in Milton Keynes, since leaving university Jessica appeared to have hopped from one teaching job to another, with spaces in between to take time off to go on marches and rallies and create general mayhem. Agatha reflected cynically that such as Jessica probably kept moving on as soon as people got used to her, as soon as she felt her power slipping. There were people like that who really did not give a fig for the environment, the whales, or anything else, but used protests as a means to gain power. Probably, thought Agatha, if she had not been killed, Jessica would soon have moved away from Dembley. She wondered what Jessica's sex life had been like. Such women often used sex as a weapon to manipulate people and gain control of them. There was a rather blurry photograph of her in one newspaper. She appeared to have been quite a striking-looking woman. There were several articles in various papers about ancient rights of way. But there was no hint at all why anyone should have wanted to murder Jessica.

At five o'clock, Agatha found her initial interest had revived. When Mrs. Mason arrived with Deborah, Agatha, going to the door and glancing in the hall mirror, wished she looked more like a great detective, whatever great detectives were supposed to look like.

Deborah, decided Agatha, seemed an inoffensive sort of girl. There were hundreds like her to be seen on the streets of any town in the Midlands—fair-haired, washed out, thin, and timid.

"So, Deborah," began Agatha, "how can I help you?"

"It's ever so worrying," said Deborah earnestly. "I don't know where to begin."

"Begin by telling me how you came to meet Sir Charles."

"It was like this. Jessica was threatening to walk across that field and she sent me to check the right of way. I didn't want to be caught out trespassing, so I called at the house first. Sir Charles was ever so nice and gave me tea. Then he asked for my phone number and then he called me up and took me out to a movie."

"Why?"

"Oh, well, *you* know . . ."

"He fancies you?"

"Maybe," said Deborah. "He seemed to like being with me."

"Has he phoned you since?"

"No, but I phoned him today and told him about you."

"So the police have released him?"

"They couldn't really keep him. The farm worker who saw him having a row with Jessica also saw him walking away towards the house when Jessica was still alive. If you're available, Sir Charles would like us both to go there for lunch tomorrow."

Agatha felt a glow of simple snobbish delight. She, Agatha Raisin, was going to have lunch at a baronet's. Stuff James! She would have great delight in telling him all about it . . . afterwards.

"Do you want to use the phone to confirm it?" asked Agatha.

"No, he said if I didn't phone back, he would know we were coming. We're expected at one."

"So do you want me to pick you up at the school? Although I feel I should not be seen by the others if I'm going to investigate this case."

"I have a little old Volkswagen. I'll get there myself," said Deborah, "and meet you there. There's one person I should warn you about. If anyone is capable of murder, he is."

"Who is that?"

"Gustav. The manservant. He doesn't like me. He told me to stay away from Sir Charles."

"And did you tell Sir Charles this?"

Deborah hung her head and muttered, "No." She hadn't wanted Sir Charles to know she was the sort of person of whom a servant disapproved.

"Don't worry," said Agatha bracingly. "No uppity servant is going to get the better of me."

Deborah opened her mouth to say that she thought Gustav could get the better of anyone, but shut it again. Let Agatha find out for herself.

Agatha went and got out a serviceable notebook and sat down again. "I'm sure you're tired of questions, Deborah. But let's go through it from the beginning."

And so in a weary little voice, Deborah described how Jessica had first arrived at the school, how she had taken over the walkers, how much they had all admired her until her reaction to Sir Charles's civil letter had seemed to go over the top and they had all decided they had had enough of her bullying ways. She went through the stories of the others, at least as much of them that she had gleaned while they had all sat around the ballroom.

"So no one except perhaps the waiters has an alibi?"

"If we had known there was going to be a murder on Saturday afternoon, then I am convinced we would have all made sure we had alibis," said Deborah with a rare show of spirit.

"Very well, then. Now this Gustav. Where does he come from? That's a German name. What's his second name?"

"I don't know," said Deborah. "No doubt the police have found out."

"Was there a detective there who looked Chinese?"

"Yes, he was present during the interviews."

Bill Wong, thought Agatha. I must try to get hold of him.

She asked Deborah a few more questions and then said she would see her on the following day. She wrote down instructions on how to get to Barfield House.

No sooner had they driven off than Agatha's doorbell sounded again. She patted her hair in the hall mirror. It would be James. Well, she might relent and forgive him for his earlier rudeness. Such news was too exciting to keep to herself. But it was Bill Wong who stood on the doorstep when Agatha opened the door. Her first sharp feeling of dismay was counteracted by the immediate thought that here was the very man she should be most glad to see.

"Come in," cried Agatha. "How's the rambler case going?"

"Now, how did you know that?"

"Because I have been asked to investigate." Agatha, leading the way through to her comfortable kitchen, reflected that she hardly ever used her sitting-room these days.

"Who by?"

"Deborah Camden."

"Why on earth did she ask you?"

Agatha bridled. "Why not? She is Mrs. Mason's niece and she had heard through her aunt of my detective work in the village."

"What can you do that the police can't?"

"Well, for a start, I've been invited to Sir Charles Fraith's for lunch tomorrow. It's easier to get to know what makes people tick when you're meeting them socially."

"I suppose so, Agatha. But you've got a way of crashing into things. The next thing we know is the murderer will be after you with a spade."

"Where did the spade come from?"

"It had been left there by the farm labourer, Joseph Noakes, the one who said he had seen Sir Charles having a row with Jessica. He's a surly chap with a big chip on his shoulder. He had been asked to clear a blockage in a ditch, had been walking back the day before, that was the Friday, got tired of carrying the spade and just stuck it among the rape at the edge of the field. There were two paths through the rape other than the mess left by Jessica. One going towards the house, which we assume was made by Sir Charles, and one leading off to the side of the field from where Jessica was struck. No footprints. Just crushed flowers."

"This Gustav," asked Agatha, "what's his background?"

"Hungarian mother, English father. Brought over here in the fifties, went into service at age fifteen in Clarence

House as a kitchen porter, then footman at the Marquess of Drent's, then started work as chauffeur, and finally butler, ending up as butler to the old man, the late Sir Charles, who died three years ago. He's fifty-two. Unblemished record."

"I always thought of butlers as being very old."

"The few that are left these days usually are. As a profession, it's finished. Gustav is a houseman, rather than butler. He never married."

"Homosexual?"

"Don't think so. All unmarried men aren't homosexual. What about me?" His eyes crinkled with amusement. "What about lover-boy, James, next door? Told him about this?"

"Not yet," said Agatha, who had no intention of recounting to Bill how she had been snubbed. "Aren't you going to tell me to keep out of it as you usually do?"

"Not this time. I don't see that a harmless lunch can put you in danger. But I'll call round here tomorrow evening. In fact, I'll be very interested to hear what you make of Sir Charles and Gustav. What did you think of Deborah?"

"Plain little girl. Not much character. Rather bowled over by the fact that Sir Charles took her out. Sort of girl easily swayed by stronger characters. I shouldn't think she had any strong political affiliation with Jessica's views. I think she just latched on to the stronger woman."

"Maybe. Anyway, I'll hear how you get on."

Logic and emotion warred in Agatha's bosom next day and emotion won. She found she was dithering over the idea of having lunch with a baronet. Logic screamed at her that Sir Charles was a mere baronet who lived in a Victorian mansion described in the guidebooks as "architecturally undistinguished." Deep down the old Agatha, product of a Birmingham slum, trembled.

Despite all the changes of dress she had put herself through, trying to find just the right outfit, she arrived at the end of the drive to Sir Charles's house a quarter of an hour early. She forced herself to park by the side of the road, and lit a cigarette while peering at her reflection in the driving mirror. There were little lines on her upper lip. She'd need to try anti-wrinkle cream. She smoked and worried and fretted until, with another look at her watch, she realized fifteen minutes had passed. With a heightened colour and a fast-beating heart, she drove up the drive.

Barfield House may have been considered "architecturally undistinguished" by the experts, but it was *big,* a huge, imposing mansion.

Deborah's car rolled to a stop just behind Agatha's and, glad of even this weak support, Agatha went to join her and together they stood on the step while Deborah rang the bell. Agatha was wearing a blouse and skirt and lamb's-wool cardigan. Deborah was wearing a pale-blue polyester trouser-suit and a little white blouse which seemed to make her more bleached-looking than ever.

The door was opened by Gustav. His black eyes flicked over them for a split second, but that look was somehow enough to demoralize both women. It seemed to say, "That I should have to open the door to such as you!"

"Sir Charles is in the sitting-room," said Gustav, leading the way across the cavernous hall.

Both women entered the sitting-room. Sir Charles rose to meet them. Sitting beside the fireplace was a faded elderly lady. Sir Charles introduced her as his aunt, Mrs. Tassy.

68

"So you're the detective," he said heartily after the introductions were over. "Brought your magnifying glass and fingerprint dust, hey?"

Simple fool, thought Agatha loftily and felt herself relax.

"Raisin," said Mrs. Tassy in a high, strangulated voice. "Would that be one of the Sussex Raisins?"

Gustav spoke from the corner of the room. "Hardly," he said.

Mrs. Tassy put on a pair of spectacles and peered at Agatha. "No, I suppose not," she said. "When are we eating, Gustav?"

"Any time you like."

Mrs. Tassy rose. She was a surprisingly tall woman. At least six feet of her loomed over Agatha. "Good," she said simply. "I'm bored."

"You won't be bored when Mrs. Raisin starts grilling us, shining lights in our faces, and applying the old rubber truncheon," said Sir Charles. "Come along, Deborah. You look as if you need fattening up."

Deborah giggled. Agatha suddenly wanted to run away. Never had she felt so timid or inadequate in years. She began to feel angry and truculent. Who the hell did these people think they were, anyway?

"Good heavens!" said Sir Charles, as they all sat round a long table in the dining-room. "Why all the silver? We can't be having that many courses."

Gustav remained silent. He poured wine. He served soup. Agatha had a feeling that he hoped she would be intimidated by the display of cutlery. But how could he have known anything about her? It must be little Deborah who was the target.

Mrs. Tassy fixed pale eyes on Agatha. "If my nephew is going to employ you, what are your fees?"

"I didn't think of charging anything," said Agatha.

"Amateur," said Gustav sotto voce from the sideboard.

Agatha swung round. "Cut the crap, you cheeky pillock," she howled.

"I do not think we are going to have a very good summer," said Mrs. Tassy into the brief startled silence which had followed Agatha's outburst. Agatha tried to remain cool but she could feel an ugly tide of red washing up her face from her neck. "I read in the paper the other day that it's something to do with the volcanic eruption in the Philippines. It is said to cause bad summers in Europe."

"It might stop you militant ramblers from frightening any more landowners," said Sir Charles, smiling fondly on Deborah.

"Oh, never tell me you are one of those." Mrs. Tassy looked curiously at Deborah. "You have to be careful. You don't want to get yourself killed."

Gustav deftly removed the empty soup plates. Agatha had been fiddling with the knives and forks beside her plate. Gustav twitched them back into place with a little sigh.

Fish in cheese sauce appeared before them next. "You're doing us proud, Gustav," said Sir Charles. "But a bit extended and formal, isn't it? I think we would have been cosier with a bit of cold pie in the kitchen."

By way of reply, Gustav raised his expressive eyebrows and retreated again to the sideboard. Agatha had a thin pearl necklace round her neck. "Are those real?" asked Mrs. Tassy.

"No," said Gustav.

Agatha tried to rally. "No one wears real pearls these days," she said. She could hear those dangerous twanging Birmingham vowels creeping to the surface of her voice.

"I do," said Mrs. Tassy, and that was the end of that subject.

"So how are you going to start detecting?" asked Sir Charles.

"I would like to see the field where the murder took place," said Agatha, and then decided to move into the attack. "Why did you tell the police that you were in London on the day of the murder?"

"Because I didn't want to be accused of it," said Sir Charles patiently.

"You panicked?"

His eyes, turned on her, were suddenly bright and intelligent. "No," he said. "I suddenly wanted to have nothing to do with all the fuss and bother. I really didn't think anyone had seen me quarrelling with that Jessica, you see."

"What were you quarrelling about?"

"Obviously about her jumping up and down in the field and wrecking the crop. She gave me a lot of stuff about being a bloated capitalist. I've never heard such clichés since I was at a meeting of the students' union at my college in Cambridge. I told her to get knotted and walked away. When I looked back, she was standing there, shouting insults at me. I thought of calling the police and then I got fed up with the whole thing. I tend to ignore things that make me fed up. Of course, now the police are thinking of charging me with obstructing them in their investigations. Such a pain."

"But surely you must have realized they would find out?"

"Why?" he asked in simple surprise. "I didn't know Noakes had such a dislike of me. None of the other estate workers would have dreamt of saying anything."

"Probably killed her himself, the silly sod," said Gustav.

"I would like that," said Mrs. Tassy meditatively.

Agatha cracked. "Yes, that would suit you lot very well," she said. "One of the farm workers being the guilty party would be just great."

"If I'd known you were going to be nasty," said Deborah, tossing her fair hair, "I'd never have asked you."

"More wine, Gustav," said Sir Charles. "You know, Mrs. Raisin, I cannot really have someone trying to help me who is prejudiced."

"I'm not prejudiced," protested Agatha. "I merely said—"

"Oh, roast beef!" exclaimed Mrs. Tassy. "You are spoiling us, Gustav."

And Agatha could think of nothing further to say. She was totally demoralized. She envied Deborah, who was happily prattling on to Sir Charles about films and books. The dreadful meal wound to its close. When Agatha, tipsy and miserable, made her way out to her car, she was well aware that nothing further had been said about engaging her services. "You shouldn't drink and drive," said Gustav as a parting shot.

Agatha drove slowly home, but not too slowly in case any of the police still searching that rape field should find the slowness of her pace suspicious.

Once home, she drank several cups of black coffee and stared miserably at the kitchen wall before going through to her sitting-room and trying ineffectually to find a television programme to take her mind off her shame. What had come over her? She, Agatha Raisin, the scourge of every maître d' from Claridges to the Ritz, had been demoralized by a pretentiously long lunch in a country mansion.

Sobered by coffee and misery, she went to answer the summons of the doorbell. Bill Wong stood there. "How'd you get on?"

"Come in," said Agatha. "Sun's out. We'll sit in the garden for a change." She made more coffee and carried two mugs out to the garden table.

"Your garden's beautiful," said Bill, looking at the glowing colours of the flowers.

"Thanks to the neighbours." Agatha glowered down into her coffee-cup.

"So what's the matter?" demanded Bill.

"I think he did it." Bill thought Agatha sounded positively pettish. "Sir Charles and that servant of his."

Bill leaned back in his chair, his almond-shaped eyes fastened on Agatha's sulky face.

"This is not like you, Agatha. Was Sir Charles high-handed with you?"

"No," muttered Agatha. "I think he's stupid and silly. He lied about not being there on Saturday and I think—"

The doorbell shrilled faintly from the front of the house. Agatha went to answer it and stared up at the tall figure of James Lacey.

"I was a bit rude to you yesterday, Agatha," he said apologetically. "I thought I was getting on fine with my writing, but then I found later that what I had written was rubbish." All the humiliations of the day forgotten for one brief glorious moment, Agatha begged him to come in and join them for coffee.

73

When James was seated at the garden table, he asked Bill, "Are you working on this rambler case?"

"Yes, and so is Agatha, or rather, so *was* Agatha," said Bill. "A girl in the case, Deborah Camden, roped our Agatha in to help Sir Charles Fraith, but Agatha seems to have come back from lunch there with a flea in both ears and won't quite tell me what went wrong."

"Odd family, the Fraiths," said James, stretching out his long legs. "So what did go wrong, Agatha?"

"It was that damned manservant, Gustav," said Agatha wearily. "He had it in for me and I got rattled."

There was a short silence while both men reflected how a rattled Agatha might behave.

"So I get the feeling Sir Charles decided he did not want your services after all, Agatha. What did you say to put him off . . . if you can think of one thing," James added, implying that Agatha might have let loose a string of insults.

"Well, he's got this odd aunt and she said it would be nice if that farm worker, Noakes, turned out to be the murderer and I said something like it suiting their type of people very well to think the hired help had done it. Sir Charles said I was prejudiced."

James laughed. "Poor old Agatha. This Gustav must be quite something to get under your skin. I know Sir Charles slightly. Friend of a young friend of mine. Oh, you must not give up detecting, Agatha. I'll speak to Sir Charles. I'll use your phone, if I may."

"If he wants me back on the case, will you come with me?" asked Agatha.

He looked down at her, his eyes twinkling. "Why not?"

"So what of your ideas that Sir Charles and Gustav are murderers?" asked Bill when James had disappeared indoors.

"Oh, I was just joking," mumbled Agatha. If James were successful, then he and she could go detecting again, and that pillock, Gustav, wouldn't matter a bit.

James got Sir Charles on the phone. "I gather you had a friend of mine, Agatha Raisin, over for lunch," he said after reintroducing himself.

"Oh, her," said Sir Charles. "That little rambler, Deborah Camden, you'll have seen her name in the papers over this business, she said this Mrs. Raisin of yours was a whiz, but I thought she was a rather odd woman with one massive chip on her shoulder."

James laughed. "She has her methods, Watson. But, by God, she gets results. Do you know how she started detecting? When she arrived first in this village, she wanted to make her mark by winning a quiche-baking competition. So she bought a quiche in London and put it in as her own. One of the judges dropped dead after eating it, so she had to find out who did it."

Sir Charles chuckled appreciatively. "Sounds like a character."

"Furthermore, Agatha and I have worked on some cases together. Don't turn her down. She's good."

"I'll try again." Sir Charles sounded suddenly weary. "Why don't both of you come over for a drink?"

"Right," said James. "What time? Sixish?"

"That'll be fine."

James returned in triumph to the garden. "I think you're on again, Agatha," he said. "We're going to Barfield House for drinks at six."

"What! This evening? I've hardly sobered up from lunch-time."

"Then drink mineral water."

James looked at Bill. "Why, no stern admonitions to keep out of it?"

Bill grinned. "Because the police are baffled. I can't see the pair of you getting into much trouble over a few drinks with Sir Charles Fraith. He's hardly likely to poison you when he's under suspicion."

Agatha looked at her watch. "It's five!" she said. "I'd better go and repair myself." She looked at James shyly. "What should I wear?"

"I don't know," said James. "We're going on business, so wear anything that's comfortable. I'll drive."

It was a different Agatha who was driven up the drive to Barfield House by James. She felt *armoured* by James. At first she had rehearsed how to explain her outburst but then decided a dignified silence on the subject would be the better policy.

Gustav opened the door to them. His eyes flicked up and down Agatha, making her feel that a plain green wool dress was not at all the thing to wear, and then led them to the sitting-room.

Sir Charles nodded to Agatha and welcomed James enthusiastically.

Gustav served drinks—Agatha stuck to mineral water—and then Sir Charles began. "We seemed to get off on the wrong foot," he said to Agatha.

"Waste of time, if you ask me," said Gustav to the panelled wall.

James's head jerked round. "Leave us alone, Gustav,"

he said sharply. "This is too important a discussion to be interrupted by your cheeky comments."

Gustav looked at Sir Charles, who nodded, and he left the room.

"How can you put up with that man?" asked James. "What's up with him?"

"He has a reputation for insolence."

"*I* haven't noticed," said Sir Charles, "and since he's my man, it's got bugger-all to do with you."

"Well, your problem." James shrugged. "Now, tell me how you got into this mess."

Agatha, now able to relax—it was just a house, after all, and Sir Charles just a man—nonetheless studied the baronet closely while he talked.

It all seemed very believable this time, now that she no longer found either him, or her circumstances, threatening. He explained at length how Gustav, returning from a visit to the keeper's cottage, had reported seeing Jessica approaching the field. Confident of soothing her, he had gone out to meet her. How had he known who she was? Deborah had described her quite accurately. When he had seen her jumping and trampling around with her great boots, he had lost his rag. He had called her a silly little girl and that had seemed to get up her nose no end, said Sir Charles with a certain amount of remembered satisfaction. Had he threatened her in any way?

For the first time Sir Charles looked uncomfortable. "There was something so arrogant, so unpleasant about her that I told her I was going to get my shotgun and blast her if she didn't get off my land. I didn't tell the police that."

"Why did you lie? Why did you say you were in London?" asked James.

"We're a very close-knit community at Barfield, the keepers, the estate workers, the farm workers—didn't know about the horrible Noakes, he was taken on recently—and I didn't brief them, I just expected them to go along with my story."

"That seems a bit naïve," commented James.

"It does now. Now I'm in a mess, and with the police looking in my direction, they aren't likely to do their job properly, which is finding out the real murderer. I've been thinking," he said earnestly, leaning back in a winged chair and cradling his glass in both hands against his chest, "I'm an easygoing sort of bod, and yet look how she riled me up. I think that lover of hers, what's-is-name, did for her. Anyway, how are you going to find out anything the police can't?"

"For a start," said Agatha, speaking for the first time, "James and I could move to Dembley, take a flat, pose as man and wife and join the Dembley Walkers. What better way is there to get to know them?"

James showed signs of alarm, but Sir Charles said enthusiastically, "What a good idea. I've some property in Dembley and I think there's a furnished flat vacant. Wait there. I'll call up my man and find out."

He went out of the room. "Agatha," said James, "you should have asked me first if I could spare the time to move to Dembley and if I wanted to pretend to be your husband."

"If you don't want to do it, don't," said Agatha.

"I didn't say that," said James. "It's just it's a big thing to do."

Agatha forced herself to remain calm. "As I said," she remarked in as even a tone as she could manage, "I'm quite prepared to go ahead on my own."

Sir Charles came back. "That's settled, then. There a jolly nice apartment in Sheep Street, bang in the center of Dembley. You can move in as soon as you like."

There was a little silence. Agatha held her breath.

"All right," said James. "I'm not getting on very far with the writing anyway."

"What are you writing?" Sir Charles asked.

"Military history."

"Which period?"

"Napoleonic wars."

"My father was a great history buff. Gustav put a lot of his books up in one of the attics. Would you like to have a rummage?"

James's eyes shone. "I'd love that."

"I'll take you up. Want to stay here, Mrs. Raisin?"

But Agatha was appalled at the idea of being left in a room which Gustav might enter, and eagerly volunteered to go with them.

When James and Agatha finally drove off together, James clutching a pile of old books, Agatha tried not to listen to his enthusiastic descriptions of the treasures he had found and how he was dying to get started writing again.

For a brief period she was to be Mrs. Lacey, albeit in name only.

But who knew what delights that could lead to!

FIVE

✝

"THAT'S an odd couple," said Jeffrey Benson a week later. It was the day after the weekly meeting of the Dembley Walkers. He was referring to a certain Mr. and Mrs. James Lacey, who had turned up and said they were eager to join the walkers. Jeffrey and the others were in the Grapes at lunch-time, a somewhat more relaxed group than they had been in previous days. All were getting used to frequent interrogations and diggings into their past by the police. Kelvin was feeling quite euphoric because the police had not discovered Jessica's visit to him or the subsequent row, and Jeffrey was beginning to feel at ease because he had not heard a word about entertaining any Irishmen.

"Bourgeois," said Alice, heaving her great bottom on the imitation medieval chair in the lounge bar. "They've got money. That was a Gucci handbag she was carrying."

"There's something a bit common about her, reelly," said Deborah, who secretly, thanks to several warm telephone calls from Sir Charles, felt she was becoming an authority on the upper classes. "He's all right, though." She giggled. "Quite attractive, I think."

"But dae we want them with us?" demanded Kelvin. "We can hardly fight the good fight wi' a couple o' Torys tagging along."

Gemma said uneasily, "Do you mean we're still going to have to face up to angry landowners, even though Jessica's dead?"

"Why not?" demanded Alice. "Jessica was a bit of a bully, but when you look at it, she had the right idea."

Deborah stared into her glass of orange juice. She suddenly did not want to be part of a group that went in for confrontations. And yet, the walkers had meant friendship and a cause. What if Sir Charles did not call her any more or want to see her? Then everything would have been for nothing, she thought sadly, and she would be alone again. She found it hard to make friends, considering the quieter, milder teachers, the ones who might be considered her own sort, not glamorous enough.

Peter Hatfield and Terry Brice unexpectedly came to Gemma's defence. "I think it's Gemma who has the right idea," said Terry. "We could have lovely walks . . ."

"Lovely walks," echoed Peter plaintively.

". . . if only we just settled down to enjoy the country-side."

Jeffrey stretched and yawned. "Oh, this Saturday should be mild enough. There's a pretty walk listed in one of the books. Most of it goes through farmland and the book says that it's well signposted."

"What year was the book published?" demanded Alice suspiciously.

"Nineteen thirties. But they update these publications,

for God's sake, or it wouldn't still be on sale. It's quite a long walk. Do we take the cars out to the beginning of it?"

But the rest decided they were proper ramblers and should walk the whole distance. They agreed to meet outside the Grapes at nine in the morning on Saturday.

"We'd better tell the Laceys," suggested Deborah.

"Where do they live?" asked Peter Hatfield.

"Got a flat in Sheep Street," said Terry. "Here"—he fished out a notebook—"I wrote it down with their phone number. That James Lacey was ever so nice to me. I'll phone him."

"Oh, suit yourself," said Peter sulkily.

It was Agatha who took the phone call later that day. She wrote down the meeting-place and the time and then went happily back to preparing a special dinner for James.

To her initial disappointment, the flat had proved to be much larger than she had anticipated, having three bedrooms. She had fantasized about there being only one bedroom. James would sleep on a cot-bed on the floor. "God, this thing's uncomfortable," he would moan. "I wish I had that nice double bed to sleep on." And Agatha would say huskily, "Why not join me?" And he would, and then, and then . . .

But all that had happened was that he took one bedroom, she had the other, and there was the third bedroom in between. Also, for the first few days, she had seen little of James, for he kept remembering things he should have brought and running back to Carsely to get them. But tonight they would have dinner together.

Agatha had bought ready-made food from Marks & Spencer, removing it from the foil dishes and putting the contents into pretty oven dishes to make it look as if she had cooked everything herself. She had candles on the table. Candle-light might be corny, but it hid the signs of ageing. How maddening that middle-aged men did not need to bother about wrinkles, or did not seem to. She had good breasts and had invested in a silk blouse with a plunging neckline and a black silk skirt which was very flattering to her somewhat still thickened figure.

As she busied herself polishing the wineglasses until they shone, she realized with a guilty little jolt that so far she had not really been doing her job properly, and that was finding out all she could about the walkers. James had gone to the local library to look through the national press files for articles on Greenham Common and see if Jessica's name had been mentioned. She, Agatha, should have been with Deborah or some of the other walkers instead of polishing wineglasses and losing herself in fantasy. Well, just this one evening. Tomorrow she would get down to work.

James was getting weary of searching the files. He had found a mention of Jessica's being arrested after cutting the wire of the perimeter fence at Greenham Common, but among the names of the other women he could not find one of any of the other walkers. He had hoped that if someone had been part of Jessica's past, there might be something there to tie her in with the murder. He sighed. It was all very far-fetched.

"We'll soon be closing up," said a voice at his elbow. He looked up and saw a pretty young librarian standing there. She had long straight blonde hair and a doll-like face. She was wearing a very short, very tight skirt and high heels.

Must cause chaos when she goes up on the ladders, he thought.

"I'll leave it," said James. "I could do with a drink."

"So could I," said the librarian.

The invitation came automatically. "Like to join me?" asked James.

She held out a hand. "My name's Mary Sprott."

"James Lacey. Where would you like to go?"

"There's a pub next door. I'll get my coat."

To do James justice, had Agatha said anything about a special dinner and that she expected him home at a certain time, he would have been there. But the last exchange with Agatha had been of the "See you this evening" variety. So, wondering in an amused way whether he looked like a dirty old man, he escorted Mary Sprott to the pub.

"I haven't seen you around Dembley before," she said. "Are you new to the town?"

"Recently arrived."

"In business?"

"No, I'm retired."

She batted her eyelashes at him. "You look ever so young to be a retired gentleman."

"Why, thank you," said James. "What would you like to drink?"

"Rum and Coke, please."

"Right, back in a moment." As James stood at the bar waiting for his order of drinks, he saw the walkers seated at a round table in the far corner. He waved to them. Peter and Terry raised limp hands. The rest just stared. Oh, dear, thought James. We're not going to get very far with that lot if they've taken a dislike to us. He wondered whether to buy them all a drink to ingratiate himself, but decided against it. He was beginning to get a feeling that he and Agatha were floundering about in an investigation which the police could do so much better with all their records and files. If Jessica had known any of them before her arrival in Dembley, then the police would soon trace it.

As he returned to Mary carrying the drinks, he saw looks of cynical amusement on the faces of the walkers and realized with a jolt that he was supposed to be a married man.

"Thanks ever so," said Mary. She leaned towards him and whispered, "You see that bunch over at that table?"

"Yes."

"That's them ramblers. It was in the papers. One of their lot was killed."

"Do you know any of them?" asked James.

"I know some of them by sight. They use the library. Weird lot. I doubt if one of them ever takes a bath."

"So what about you?" asked James. "It must be a lovely job, working in a library, all those books."

She shrugged. "It's a job. Gets a bit boring."

"I suppose it does," said James, thinking she must be only in her early twenties. "Who are your favourite authors?"

"I don't read much. I prefer the telly."

James tried to hide his shock. "But my dear girl, what's the point of becoming a librarian if you have no interest in books?"

"Mum said it was a good job," said Mary. "It's like this, I've got ever such a good memory, so I did well at school. Mum said being a librarian was nicer than working in a shop. With a memory like mine, I'm good at it. I can remember where everything is."

"But don't some of the people who come in ask your advice on what books to read?"

"I turn them over to old Miss Briggs. She reads everything, but she can't remember where the books are, so we make a good team."

"So what would you like to do?" asked James, becoming bored.

"I'd like to be an air hostess. See a bit of the world."

"Another drink?" asked James.

"Yes, please. I'm ever so hungry."

For the first time, James thought uneasily of Agatha. "Do they do food here?"

"They do a good steak-and-kidney pie."

"All right. I'll make a phone call first." James went and dialed the flat but there was no reply. Agatha was probably out investigating. He returned to the table. He might as well have something to eat. Then he might get rid of her and go and join the walkers. That's what Agatha would do.

"I still say there's something odd about the Laceys," said Alice. "That's the girl from the library he's with, and I'll tell you something else. He doesn't look married. Do you think they could be police infiltrating our group in order to spy on us?"

"Oh, that's ridiculous," said Deborah. She suddenly wanted to go home. Charles might be calling her. In her mind, it was no longer Sir Charles. She was unnerved by the conversation about the "Laceys." What if they were challenged by the group and confessed that it was she who had brought the vipers into their midst? A thin film of sweat formed on her upper lip. Kelvin thumped another drink down in front of her and she groaned inwardly. As soon as she had finished it, she would make her escape.

Agatha stood outside the library. But it was firmly closed for the night. Where could James be? She turned and looked about her. There was a pub across the road called the Grapes. She registered in her mind that that was where they were to gather on the Saturday for their ramble and then wondered if James had gone there for a drink.

She walked across the road to the pub and pushed open the door of the lounge bar. The first sight that met her eyes was that of James sitting with a pretty blonde. Both were eating steak-and-kidney pie. The blonde threw back her head and laughed at something James was saying. Her short skirt had ridden right up. Black rage boiled up in Agatha. She was to reflect ruefully afterwards that she must have gone insane. For in that moment, she *became* Mrs. Lacey.

"What the hell do you think you're doing here, James?" she demanded in a loud voice. There was a silence in the pub.

"Oh, hullo, *dear,*" said James, his face flaming. "This is Miss Sprott, the librarian. Miss Sprott, my wife."

Determined to get revenge on James and hating every inch of Mary Sprott, from her long legs to her blonde hair, Agatha departed into the realms of fantasy.

"Have you forgotten our anniversary?" she demanded. "I prepared a special dinner. I *slaved* all day over it, and what do I find? You sitting here having ghastly pub grub with some tart."

"How dare you, you old bat?" screeched Mary.

Agatha's bearlike eyes bored into Mary's. "Just get this straight, sweetie," she said. "This is my husband, so you keep your grubby little hands off him."

Mary burst into tears, scrabbled for her handbag on the floor beside her chair, seized it, and fled the pub.

"Let's get out of here," said James, his face grim. "No, not another word, Agatha. You're a disgrace."

The walkers, open-mouthed, watched them go.

"Well," marvelled Kelvin, "if they're no' married, then I'm a Dutchman's uncle."

"Poor bugger," said Jeffrey. "Let's be nice to him on Saturday."

Deborah heaved a tiny sigh of relief, excused herself, and slipped quietly out of the pub and went to phone Sir Charles.

Agatha had never seen James so angry. In vain did she try to say that she had simply been putting on an act. "And," raged James, "I am packing up and leaving. I will not tolerate such behaviour."

Agatha, now completely at a loss for words, followed him upstairs to the flat. As they entered, the phone was ringing. James answered it. It was Sir Charles Fraith.

"Congratulations to Agatha Raisin on a great performance," chuckled Sir Charles. "She's turning out to be as good as you said she was."

"What do you mean?" demanded James sharply.

"Deborah's just called me. Those ramblers were talking in the pub about how you two didn't look married and that they thought you were both police spies, and then our Agatha turns up and puts on the best angry marital scene

Deborah says she's ever witnessed. Went down like a charm."

"Oh," said James, looking round in amazement at Agatha. "I didn't realize . . . I mean, yes, she's very good at it."

"Call me when you learn anything," said Sir Charles cheerfully. "I am still suspect numero uno."

When James had said goodbye, he turned to Agatha and said in a mild voice, "I am so sorry, Agatha. I should have let you explain. I didn't know you were acting. That was Sir Charles. Deborah told him that the walkers didn't think we were man and wife and were beginning to think we were police spies, but after your scene, they were convinced we were what we claimed to be. You knew this, of course. I should have let you explain."

"Of course," said Agatha weakly. She waved her hand at the table. "I don't suppose you want any dinner."

"On the contrary," he said cheerfully, "you didn't give me time to get more than a few mouthfuls in the pub."

"Be back in a minute," said Agatha and scurried off to the bathroom, where she indulged in a hearty bout of tears caused by a mixture of shame and relief.

When she had served dinner, she was so sensible and composed that James was once more intrigued by the investigation. They both decided to try to find out from the walkers' neighbours anything they could about Jessica— had she been seen with any of them—or rowed with any of them—before the murder?

James said he would try Kelvin, and Agatha said she would check on Deborah.

"Why Deborah?" asked James.

"I've been thinking," said Agatha, "she might have

called us in to divert suspicion from herself."

"Seems a bit far-fetched, but I suppose we have to try everything."

Later that night, Deborah sat in Burger King in the main street of Dembley with Sir Charles Fraith. He had suggested a late supper. Deborah looked around her and thought of all the posh restaurants people ate in, hoping to dine alongside people like Charles.

But he listened with such interest when she talked of her work in the school and of the pupils. "That's an odd bunch you've got in with," remarked Sir Charles.

"Oh, you mean the Dembley Walkers. It's something to do."

"Are you going out this Saturday?"

"Yes, I have to keep an eye on our detectives."

"Pity. I've got people at the weekend and wanted to ask you over."

Deborah spilled some coffee from her polystyrene cup. Damn the walkers. Should she say she would drop going with them? Would that look too eager? Would . . . ?

"Of course, if you're all through by the evening, you can come for dinner," she realized he was saying.

"What time?"

"Oh, eight for eight-thirty."

"Thanks awfully."

"My pleasure. Only hope you don't find it a bore. Gosh, I'm tired. Have you got your car?"

"No, I live quite close by."

"Then I'll walk you home."

Dembley was an old market town which no longer boasted a market but sometimes on calm evenings still held

91

a flavour of the old days. The market hall with its splendid arches and clock tower now housed an Italian restaurant and an auction room. The beautiful seventeenth-century house opposite had a garish neon sign in one window flashing out CHINESE TAKE-AWAY. Concrete blocks of shops nearly blocked off the view of the thirteenth-century church. White-faced youths leaned against lamp-posts at street corners and jeered at the world in a tired way, their speech liberally sprinkled with obscenities.

As they passed one group, a thin teenager shouted out, "Getting your leg over tonight, guv?" and the rest sniggered.

To Deborah's horror, Sir Charles stopped dead in his tracks. "Why did you say that?" he demanded, addressing the teenager.

The boy looked at his shoes and muttered, "Sod off."

Sir Charles stared at him curiously. Then he turned to Deborah and took her arm. "It's not that they suffer from material poverty," he said. "It's a poverty of the mind, wouldn't you say?"

Deborah, head down, muttered, "Oh, ignore them. They might have knives."

Sir Charles turned back. "Have you got knives?" he asked.

For some reason, his simple, almost childlike curiosity appeared to embarrass the youths more than a stream of insults would have done.

Muttering, they slid off, still in a group, used to being in a gang since they were toddlers, frightened to break away from each other and become vulnerable individuals.

"Here's where I live," said Deborah, stopping in front of a dark doorway between a dress shop and an off-licence.

"Would you . . . would you like to come up for a cup of coffee?"

Unnoticed by Deborah, who was studying her shoes, a predatory gleam entered Sir Charles's eyes. He fancied her a lot, he thought. She was different from the girls he usually escorted. There was something so pliant and appealing about her thinness and whiteness. He was not used to shy women and found Deborah a novelty. "Not tonight," he said. He took her face between his hands and kissed her on the lips. "See you Saturday. Would you like me to send Gustav for you?"

"No!" said Deborah. "I mean, I know the way."

"And so you do. 'Bye."

Deborah scurried up the stairs, her heart beating hard. She was going to be a dinner guest at Barfield House. She telephoned her mother in Stratford-upon-Avon. Mrs. Camden, a tired, faded woman, worn out with years of work in looking after Deborah and her two brothers because Mr. Camden had shot off for parts unknown shortly after Deborah, the youngest, had been born, listened to Deborah's excited voice bragging about how she was going to be a dinner guest at Barfield House.

"Make sure your underwear's clean," cautioned Mrs. Camden. "You never know what might happen."

And Deborah knew her mother did not mean that her daughter should be prepared for a night of lust but was simply expressing an old fear that one of her children might meet with an accident and arrive at the hospital in dirty underwear.

The next morning Agatha did not rush to get to the kitchen first to make a wifely breakfast. She was appalled at her behaviour of the night before. She was determined to back off and play it cool. So she mentally shelved all her earlier plans of cooking up breakfast in a hurriedly bought satin nightgown and negligé, and bathed and dressed in a plain skirt and blouse and sensible shoes.

When she arrived in the kitchen, James was cooking eggs and bacon. "I put some on for you," he said over his shoulder. "Sit down and I'll serve you. There's coffee in the jug."

Agatha saw the morning newspapers lying at the side of the table and looked hurriedly through them all. But there was no news of the rambler murder.

James served her and himself, ate hurriedly and then settled down to read a newspaper, allowing Agatha to reflect that this was probably more like real married life than any of her wild imaginings.

She finished eating and cleared away the dirty plates into the dishwasher. The flat, although expensively furnished, depressed her. It was the sort of place that reminded her of her London days, when she had allowed decorators to do the job for her and never revealed any of her own personality in the furnishings. She wished suddenly she had brought her cats with her. They were back in the care of Doris Simpson. Perhaps she would take a run home and collect them. She was sure James would not mind.

"So what are you going to do today?" asked James finally.

"I'm going to where Deborah lives," said Agatha. "I'll take a clipboard and say I'm a market researcher."

"That's a good idea. But don't you think it might be easier just to question Mrs. Mason?"

"I want to find out Deborah's movements before the

94

murder. Mrs. Mason won't know that."

"But won't people think it odd that a market researcher would want to know about Deborah Camden?"

"Not the way I go about it. Look, you represent some product and suggest there's going to be a prize. They invite you in for a cup of tea. Once in, you start talking about the murder."

James looked thoughtfully at Agatha, as if debating whether she was the type of woman that people asked in for a cup of tea, but he said, "I'll see what I can find out about Kelvin. We'll meet up back here early evening, swap notes, and then go to that restaurant where Peter and Terry work." He retreated back into his newspaper while Agatha's feverish mind planned what to wear to dinner.

Seeing she was going to get no more conversation out of James, Agatha found a clipboard among her belongings, attached several sheets of paper to it, and set out.

When she arrived at the doorway between the shops which led to the flats above, one of which was Deborah's, Agatha longed for the pre-security days when one just opened the street door and walked in. She studied the names on the bells: D. Camden, Wotherspoon, Sprott—her eyes narrowed—and Comfrey.

After a little hesitation, she rang the bell marked "Wotherspoon." No intercom. The buzzer went and Agatha quickly pushed open the street door and went in and up a shabby flight of uncarpeted wooden stairs. An elderly man leaning on a stick was standing on the landing peering down at her as she made her ascent. "I don't know you," he said. "If you're selling something, I'm not interested."

Agatha pinned a bright smile on her face and went resolutely on up. "I am doing some market research about the tea-drinking habits of the English. It will only take a moment of your time."

He had a grey, very open-pored face, loose dentures, and thin hair greased in streaks across a narrow head. He was wearing a grey shirt and grey trousers and carpet slippers of a furry plum-coloured fabric, very new, probably a present from some grandchild, thought Agatha.

"Questions, questions," he grumbled. "I don't want to answer damn-fool questions."

"We are paying ten pounds to each person who helps us," said Agatha, all bright efficiency.

"Oh!" His truculence melted. "Come in. As a matter of fact, I was just about to have a cup of tea."

Agatha followed him into a sparsely furnished living-room. There was a photograph of him in army uniform taken during World War II, when he was a young man. He had been very handsome. Age, it comes to all of us, thought Agatha, repressing a shudder. There was another photograph, a wedding one. "That your wife?" asked Agatha, pointing at it.

"Yes, she passed on fifteen years ago. Cancer. Odd, that," remarked Mr. Wotherspoon, peering blearily at the photograph. "I always thought Madge would see me out."

"You must miss her."

"What's that? Oh, no, she was an old bitch."

Agatha blinked but tactfully said nothing. He poured two dark cups of tea into chipped mugs. He added tinned sweetened condensed milk to his own and held the tin over Agatha's cup. "No, no," she said hurriedly. "Now just a few questions."

"Where's the money?" he asked.

Agatha fished out a ten-pound note and gave it to him. She was sitting down at a scarred living-room table as he bent over her to take it. It was then she smelt him. He smelt very strongly of rum.

He sat down next to her and put a gnarled hand on her knee. Agatha picked it up and said roguishly, "Naughty, naughty." He leered at her and put his hand back again.

"I'll take that money back if you don't behave yourself," said Agatha sharply. The hand was removed.

Agatha asked a few questions—age, job, taste in tea, how many cups, where did he buy it, and so on. At last she felt she had put on a good-enough act and said, "I would love another cup of tea, if you can spare the time. I don't get to meet very many interesting people."

"No, there's not many good uns left," he said. He poured her another cup of tea and then sank into an old man's reminiscences, his voice droning on in the stuffy room like a fly trapped against the glass of a window.

When he said, "Ah, young people these days . . ." Agatha interrupted with, "That rambling murder, talking about young people these days. You've got one of them living next door."

"That skinny little thing! At least she didn't murder anyone. Couldn't say 'boo' to a goose, that one couldn't."

"Many boy-friends?"

He leaned forward and winked. "Not her. She's one of them homosapens."

Agatha digested this and translated it quickly in her brain.

"Do you mean she's homosexual . . . I mean, a lesbian?"

97

"I caught the pair of them in each other's arms. I'm telling you. I've seen a thing or too. I 'member when we was in Tunis—"

"Never mind Tunis," interrupted Agatha. "What pair?"

"Her, Deborah, and that one wot was killed, arms round each other, they had."

"Where was this?"

"Out on the stairs."

"But a lot of women hug each other."

"But they was kissing and groaning."

"Did you tell the police this?"

"Not me. Hadn't the time to spend with me even though I told them I was an old soldier. No, all they wants to know is if I'd heard her or seen her having a row with that Jessica and I hadn't seen a blind thing. I mostly keeps meself to meself."

"So when did you see them hugging and kissing?"

"Reckon about a month ago. I tell you, what the world is coming to these days, I don't know."

Agatha stood up. "You've been most helpful, Mr. Wotherspoon."

"Won't you stay?" Loneliness peered out from old eyes. "We could have a natter."

Much as she thought him horrible, Agatha nonetheless felt guilty as she made her way to the door, said goodbye firmly and went down the stairs and out into the freedom of the sunny street. She wondered how James was getting on.

James privately would have liked to think up some idea for interviewing people that was different from Agatha's. But at last he decided that a market researcher was as good as anything. He had no fear of being seen by Kelvin. Like the others, he would be at work.

Kelvin lived in a tower block near the school, a depressing place surrounded by scrubby grass and litter. What trees there were stood semi-shattered, raising their few remaining branches up to the sky. There were other signs of vandalism everywhere, and he found that the lift was out of order and had probably been out of order for some time, for the sign saying so was covered with old graffiti.

Kelvin lived on the tenth floor. James decided that the police would have interrogated the neighbours on either side of his flat and wondered if he might have better luck questioning the people underneath, as sounds carried down the way.

At the first flat he met with no success at all, perhaps because he never thought of Agatha's idea of offering money. He said he was doing a survey about which kind of washing detergent was most used in Dembley. A sour-faced woman simply slammed the door in his face. He tried the next door after squinting upwards and deciding it must be the one directly under Kelvin's.

The door was opened by a tired-looking woman in her thirties. Her dyed blonde hair was showing an inch of dark roots and her heavy make-up looked like yesterday's.

"It's not the poll-tax, is it?" she asked nervously.

"No," said James. "I would like to ask you some questions about which soap powder you use."

To his relief, she gave a little jerk of her head. "Come in."

He walked through a minuscule hall and into a living-room full of cheap furniture, all of which seemed to be falling apart. The sofa had been slashed, an arm was off one chair, and the table looked as if someone had recently tried to cleave it with an axe.

"My husband," she said, following his eyes. "He do go on something awful when he has the drink in him."

"Where is he now?" asked James nervously.

"Out on the building site. Come into the kitchen, will you? I'm not much use. I just buy the first packet I see in the supermarket."

He followed her into a small kitchen, averting his eyes from the smashed cupboards, no doubt signs of the absent husband's drunken wrath. She pulled a packet of soap powder from a cupboard under the sink and held it up. "This any good?"

He proceeded to ask questions—number in family, how often clothes were washed, and so on—automatically writing down the answers, wondering how to introduce the subject of the tenant upstairs. "I'm sorry to take up so much of your time," he ventured politely.

She gave him a flirtatious smile. "I don't mind. Don't get to see much people. Like a cup of tea?"

"Yes, please," said James, smiling back.

He leaned against the kitchen counter while she plugged in an electric kettle. He looked down from the window. From down below came the harsh cries of little children trying to catch a cat to torture it. The cat escaped. The children hunched together as if plotting further horrors and then they ran off, screaming at nothing.

"Been doing this job long?" he realized she was asking.

"I'm retired. I do bits for the company a few times a year. Free-lance. I'm not on the payroll."

The kettle boiled. She filled a small teapot after putting in six tea-bags, arranged a bottle of milk, a bag of sugar,

100

and two mugs on a tin tray with the teapot, and carried them into the living-room.

The tea was very strong indeed. She leaned back on the battered sofa and crossed her legs. She had very good legs. In fact, thought James, she had probably been a pretty girl before marriage knocked the stuffing out of her, much as the stuffing was spilling out of the sofa on which she sat.

"You've had a bit of excitement around here," said James, sipping his tea and trying not to shudder.

"How come?"

"Isn't one of your neighbours one of those ramblers, a Scotsman?"

"Oh, him." She jerked a thumb at the ceiling. "Lives up above."

"Look like a murderer?"

"Too soft, I'd say. Once tried to come on to me." She recrossed her legs and adjusted her skirt so that a bit of grimy lace showed underneath. "But I wasn't interested. He's that kind, you know. Fancies himself as a lady's man. I don't think he can get it up."

"That's a bit harsh, surely," said James. "You can't tell that by looking at him."

She giggled. "I can tell by listening. Should have heard her going at it."

"Who?"

"Some woman he had with him."

"When was this?" asked James sharply.

"I dunno. Oh, yeah, it was before that murder, a few days before. Round about midnight. My old man was passed out, and I was thinking, what a life, listening to the bed creaking upstairs. I mean, you can hear everything in these flats. Then I heard them shouting. Then I heard someone thumping about. Then going towards the door. Curiosity was killing me, so I went to our front door and opened it a crack. I heard her outside, shouting, "You can't even make it and you know why? You're probably a closet faggot."

"Did you get a look at her?"

"Naw."

"Pity."

"Why?"

"It would be interesting to know if she was that woman that got murdered."

She looked at him round-eyed and then, to his horror, she darted over to where he was sitting and sank down on his lap, "Oh, I'm so frightened," she murmured into his hair.

Oh, Agatha, Agatha, thought James. I wish you were here. And then a key grated in the lock. She was off his lap and back on the sofa with her skirt demurely pulled down about her knees as a huge burly man lurched into the room. "Who's this?" he roared.

"One of those men doing market research," she said.

He jerked his thumb at the door. "Out!" he shouted. And James was up and out the door and down the stairs as fast as he could.

Agatha was beginning to feel a bit sulky. She and James were seated that evening in the Copper Kitchen being served by Terry Brice. The initial excitement of sharing their discoveries was over. James kept talking about the case when Terry was out of earshot, and Agatha, who had been writing romantic scripts for him all day, could not understand why he wasn't speaking any of the lines. She wrenched herself into reality with an effort when he said, "We should tell Bill Wong about this."

"Couldn't we wait just a little?" said Agatha. "I mean, he might order us to keep clear."

"I don't know about that. We're private citizens. He can't stop us living in Dembley or going out with the ramblers. I sympathize with you, because we're certainly suffering in the cause, having to pretend to be man and wife"—Agatha winced—"and eating this quite dreadful food. Leave it, Agatha. I'll make us an omelette when we get home. What is that you're poking your fork in?"

"It said on the menu it was old-fashioned Irish stew. How's your steak?"

"Like army boots." He signalled to Terry. "Take this away. We can't eat any more of it."

"Why?" he asked plaintively.

"For a start," said Agatha, "this Irish stew is disgusting. The gravy's lukewarm and there doesn't seem to be much meat and there's too much salt."

"We *are* fussy, aren't we, sweetie. That's Jeffrey's favourite dish." Terry's eyes glinted maliciously. "But then, he likes all things Irish."

"What's that supposed to mean?" asked James.

Terry leaned one slim hip on the edge of the table. "Haven't you heard our Jeffrey on the subject of Free Ireland? Quite fiery, he is." Peter Hatfield sailed up. "What are you lot gossiping about?"

"They don't like the food," said Terry.

"Fussy, fussy," chided Peter. "You going on this walk on Saturday?"

"Yes," said James. "How can you pair get the time off on Saturday? I mean, that must be your busy day."

"We don't work Saturdays. I know it's odd, but they were so keen to have a couple of waiters who would do Sundays that they let us off."

"So how come you were both here on the day of the murder?" asked James and then cursed himself as Terry's eyes narrowed suspiciously. "How did you know that?" he asked.

"Someone said something about it at your meeting," said Agatha quickly. "That fair girl, Deborah what's-her-name."

"Considering she's prime suspect number one, she should watch her mouth," said Terry waspishly.

"Why is she prime suspect?"

"Because," said Terry patiently, as if speaking to an idiot, "she was the last one to see Jessica alive."

"What?" Agatha stared at him. "But she said she was window-shopping."

"Well, one of our customers, a Mrs. Hardy, she said as how she saw Deborah's car heading out of Dembley to the Barfield estate on that Saturday, and if she wasn't going to see Jessica, where was she going?"

SIX

†

JAMES, the following morning, finally agreed to Agatha's suggestion that she should talk directly to Alice and Gemma and see what she could find out and James should talk to Jeffrey, and after that, they would tell Bill Wong what they knew. As neither of the people they wanted to interview was likely to be free before early evening, they decided to spend the day in Carsely, attending to household chores.

Neither had realized what an amount of gossip their taking off together for parts unknown would cause in the village, Mrs. Mason having kept discreetly quiet.

Agatha's first caller after she had fed her cats was the vicar's wife, Mrs. Bloxby.

"And where have you been?" asked Mrs. Bloxby.

"We just went off on a little trip," said Agatha, rather proud of the fact that the vicar's wife obviously thought she and James were now "a number."

Mrs. Bloxby's kind eyes surveyed Agatha's flushed and

happy face. "You like Mr. Lacey, do you not?"

"Oh, yes, we're great friends."

They were sitting in Agatha's garden. The cats rolled on the lawn in the sunlight. Great fleecy clouds ambled across the sky overhead. It was an idyllic day.

"I sometimes think," said the vicar's wife, leaning back in her chair and addressing a cloud, "that we are very quick to counsel young people while neglecting our contemporaries."

"Meaning?" asked Agatha.

Mrs. Bloxby's mild eyes descended again to rest on Agatha's face. "Meaning that a lot of the old advice is still relevant in this wicked age, even for women such as ourselves. I have observed that men who get what they want outside marriage, particularly confirmed bachelors like James Lacey, are therefore content to stay unmarried."

"I am not having an affair with James," snapped Agatha.

"Oh, my dear, I thought . . . You must forgive me for jumping to the wrong conclusion." Mrs. Bloxby gave a little laugh. "I should have realized—you are probably both investigating something. Do forgive me."

"That's all right," mumbled Agatha, "but don't tell anyone in the village we're on a case. It's supposed to be a secret."

"I should have known better. Do not think me impertinent. Mr. Lacey is a very charming man. But he did have an affair with poor Mary, that woman who was murdered, and in that case I always thought it was a matter of casual sex."

No, thought Agatha, he was briefly in love with her, and remembered sharply all the pain she had felt.

As Mrs. Bloxby began to talk of village matters, Agatha suddenly wished she herself had not been so honest. She wanted every woman in the village to think that she was having an affair with James. But now Mrs. Bloxby, without revealing anything about the investigation, would contrive to let everyone know the friendship was innocent.

After the vicar's wife had left, Agatha decided to take herself down to Moreton-in-Marsh for a quiet lunch. She wanted to be alone and think about James and turn over everything he had said in her mind, always searching for some hint that his feelings might be warming towards her.

Moreton-in-Marsh is a busy Cotswold market town with a wide tree-lined main street on the Fosse Way, an old Roman military road. Ever since the Abbot of Westminster, who owned the land, decided to make use of the transport on the Fosse Way and a new Moreton was built in 1222, it has always been a favourite stopping place for travellers, the wool merchants of medieval times being replaced with tourists.

Agatha found a parking place after some difficulty. Even in the depths of winter, it is hard to find a parking place in Moreton, where the number of cars and the absence of people often puzzled Agatha. Where did so many car owners go? There wasn't enough work or enough shops to draw them all. Agatha went into the tourist information centre to see if she could pick up some pamphlets about rambling walks to take along on Saturday in order to show the Dembley Walkers she was a dedicated member. She read a tourist pamphlet on Moreton-in-Marsh to see if there was something about the old town she did not know. And there was. One pamphlet explained that the charter for the market had been granted by King Charles I in 1638. "Some years later," she read, "he stayed at the White Hart

107

Royal, which was a well-known Coaching Inn, and was part of the Trust House Forte Hotel Group." Agatha had a brief and vivid picture of King Charles and his Cavaliers with their booted feet up on the hotel tables listening to the piped Muzak which is a feature of Trust House Forte Hotels.

After a look in a thrift shop, she went to the White Hart and ate a massive plate of lamb stew. She emerged later blinking into the sunlight, drugged with food, feeling the waistline of her skirt uncomfortably tight.

Was there something about women of a certain age, she wondered, that, when they wanted to attract a man, instead of getting on the exercise bicycle, they stuffed themselves with food?

For his part, James had had a bar lunch at the Red Lion and had endured a lot of sly teasing of the what-have-you-been-doing-with-our-Agatha variety. As he walked home, he wondered whether Agatha's reputation was being damaged and then decided it was not. Provided there was no truth in the rumours, they would soon die out.

He found he was anxious to get on with the investigation, and as he walked down Lilac Lane, he saw Agatha getting out of her car and hailed her. "I think we'd better get going," he said. "I want to bump into Jeffrey as he comes out of the school as if by accident and take him for a drink. What about you?"

"I'll just knock on Alice's front door and say I've come to ask her advice about boots," said Agatha, feeling lethargic and heavy and wishing she had not eaten so much.

She fell asleep in the car—they had used her car for the journey back to Carsely and James was driving it—and awoke to hear James saying in an amused voice, "I didn't know you snored, Agatha."

"Sorry," she said. "Had too much to eat at lunch."

She wished she could always look and feel bandbox-fresh for him. She felt old and began to worry about those wrinkles on her upper lip. Surely they hadn't been there before she went to London. That's what PR did for you, she thought sadly. James had very good eyesight. When he looked at her, she could feel his blue eyes fastening on those wrinkles. How could a man want to kiss any woman with those nasty little wrinkles above her mouth?

Agatha did not know that James felt most at ease with her when she was quiet and crushed. She felt she had to be always "on stage" for him.

He dropped her off near Alice's and went on to their own flat, leaving the car outside and setting out on foot for the school.

Children of all shades were tumbling out of the school gates. He still found it strange to hear Indian and Pakistani children calling to each other in broad Midlands accents. Although their faces did not have the pinched, white, unhealthy appearance of the native British, they held that flat, discontented look of the underprivileged.

He saw Jeffrey strolling out and drew back a little and then began to follow him. Finally James speeded up and crossed a busy street to the other side, crossed back again, and came face to face with Jeffrey and hailed him. "Hot day," said James. "Care for a drink?"

"All right," said Jeffrey. James noticed Jeffrey no longer eyed him with suspicion. The reason for that soon came out when they were seated in a pub called the Fleece, Jeffrey saying he was tired of the crowd at the Grapes.

"You shouldn't let that wife of yours wear the trousers," said Jeffrey, raising a pint of bitter. "Cheers."

James was about to protest but then decided that the role of hen-pecked husband was putting him in a sympathetic light. "Oh, I don't know," he said easily. "I suppose when you've been married as long as we have, you get so you don't notice it. But I would have judged you to favour equal rights for women."

"Equal rights, yes," said Jeffrey moodily, "but not domination."

"Was Jessica like that, the dead woman?" asked James. And then added quickly, "Sorry, I forgot you were close to her."

Jeffrey shrugged. "She was a convenient lay," he said. "But then, you never can tell with women. They say they're liberated, they say they only want sex, and the next thing they're pushing you around. What that wife of yours needs is a good punch in the mouth."

"But if you advocate rights for women, then you shouldn't be advocating punches in the mouth," said James.

"Why not? They consider themselves equal to men, then treat them like men. If a man gives you any lip, you sock him one. Why not sock a woman?"

"Apt to end up in prison," said James.

"Then just walk away from it. I'll never get married." Jeffrey flexed his muscles. "Plenty of crumpet out there."

James suddenly found himself disliking Jeffrey intensely. He had heard of such men but had never met one before, the type who claim to hold liberal views and underneath hold the same views as any American redneck. Liberal views on women as held by the Jeffreys of this world were simply a convenient way of talking some woman into bed and having sex without responsibility.

With a conscious effort, he forced himself to laugh, man to man.

"Who do you think murdered Jessica?" he asked.

"I think it was one of the women," said Jeffrey. "Our Jessica was bi-sexual. Alice was jealous of her because she was after Gemma. Then she messed about a bit with our Deborah, and God knows what she got up to with Mary. I mean, think about Mary. She was probably the last one to see Jessica alive. That business about having food poisoning! She could have made that up to give herself an alibi."

"And do the police suspect you?" asked James. "I mean, you being her lover and all that."

"They probably still do. But I didn't do it, so they can ask all the questions they like. Do you know the filth even searched my flat? 'What are you looking for?' I asked them. 'A spade?' "

"I'm surprised," ventured James, "that you don't think Sir Charles did it."

A sneer marred Jeffrey's face. "That sort don't even fart without asking permission from the police. Besides, he's got lots of people there to do the dirty for him. But I think it was a woman. Women are vicious." He looked pointedly at his empty tankard, and James quickly ordered another.

"Oh, well, let's talk about something else," said James. "I'm thinking of settling in Ireland."

"Which part?" asked Jeffrey sharply.

"The south, of course. I write books, or try to write books, anyway. My mother's Irish," lied James. "Do you

111

know, if you're a writer you don't have to pay taxes?"

"Yes, grand country, so it is." Jeffrey's Midlands accent had faded, to be replaced by a slightly Irish one.

"The only trouble," said James, handing money over the bar for the drinks, "is that writer friends tell me that the IRA come calling and tell the writer that since he's not paying taxes, he can jolly well pay towards the Cause."

"And why not?" demanded Jeffrey truculently. "Why should they live off the fat of the land and not pay for it?"

"I suppose you have a point," said James, wondering what it would be like to punch Jeffrey in the mouth.

Agatha took a quick look around Alice's flat while Alice was in the kitchen making coffee. There was distinct evidence of two contrasting personalities. The bookshelves were divided between heavy political tomes and paperback romances. On the low coffee-table was stacked *Marxism Today* alongside *Women's Weekly*. There was a pottery wheel over by the window and a large stuffed pink teddy bear sat on the sofa.

Alice came back in carrying two cups of coffee. She smiled at Agatha. "I'm glad you've come to me for advice about boots, but I've got a surprise for you. Not boots—trainers, or sneakers, as our American cousins call them. Like these." She stuck out a foot. Agatha wondered why great white trainers on female feet should look so threatening. "They'll set you back about forty pounds," boomed Alice. "But worth every penny. I can walk for miles and never get sore feet. Why did you want to join us?"

"Why do you think?" Agatha ruefully patted her waistline. "I find jogging too energetic, and a walk in the country is just the thing for getting my weight down and seeing a bit of the scenery. The trouble with driving every-where is that one might as well be in London. It's hard to appreciate the countryside when all you ever see of it is trees and fields whizzing past the car windows."

"Not to mention adding to the pollution problem," said Alice. "Jessica always said . . ." Her eyes filled with tears, and she turned her head away and said gruffly, "Sorry, I still miss her."

"It must have been a great blow to you," murmured Agatha.

"It's the guilt, you see." Alice took out a man's hand-kerchief and gave her nose a vigorous blow. "She came here looking for a bed and I threw her out. I thought she was after my Gemma. If only we had all stayed friends, we would have gone with her and this terrible murder would never have happened."

"Who do you think did it?" asked Agatha.

"Oh, Sir Charles Fraith. But being who he is, we'll never see justice done. There's one law for the rich and another for the poor. He lied about being in London when she was killed. He was seen threatening her, but he'll pull all sorts of strings and we'll never hear another word about it."

"Don't you think it might have been Jeffrey Benson?" ventured Agatha. "He seems to have been her lover."

"How did you know that?"

"Gossip at the walkers' meeting," said Agatha.

"Humph. The bourgeois lack of loyalty among that lot sometimes amazes me. No, I don't think Jeffrey did it, but the police will want to pin it on him so that their dear Sir Charles will escape scot-free. Oh, here's Gemma."

Gemma walked in. She gave Agatha a sidelong smile.

"What have you got there?" asked Agatha, looking at

113

a couple of videos that Gemma was carrying.

"I thought we might watch these tonight," said Gemma. "I've got *Mad Maniac* and *Serial Passion*."

Alice sighed. "I'm not going to watch that American rubbish."

"Suit yourself," said Gemma. "Any chocky biccies?"

"In the tin over there," said Alice with a weak, indulgent smile. "Such a child," she whispered to Agatha.

Gemma caught Agatha's eye and winked. Agatha began to wonder about Gemma. Who exactly was this little shop-girl who went in for a lesbian affair and liked watching videos about serial killers? She remembered from the reviews that the two films Gemma had chosen to watch were particularly nasty.

But Alice had caught that wink and she suddenly stood up and loomed over Agatha. "I don't want to hurry you off," she said, "but I've got a lot to do."

"Of course." Agatha got to her feet as well. "See you Saturday."

Agatha was glad to get out of there. On reflection, she decided that there was something quite frightening about Alice and Gemma.

She and James were just having a cup of coffee and sharing notes when there was a ring at the doorbell. James went to open the door and found Bill Wong standing there. He came in and looked thoughtfully about him.

"What are you two up to?" he demanded. "And don't tell me it's because you've decided to shack up together. You could have done that in Carsely."

"Sit down, Bill," said Agatha. "We were going to phone you. I told you Deborah Camden had asked me to investigate the case on behalf of Sir Charles. Wait till you hear what we found out."

He listened, his face growing grim as they reeled off the new evidence they had found: Kelvin had had a row with Jessica; Deborah had been seen driving out of Dembley on the Saturday afternoon in the direction of the Barfield estate; Peter and Terry never usually worked on Saturday afternoons and yet had opted to work the Saturday of the murder; and Jeffrey Benson appeared to be an IRA sympathizer.

"And how long were you going to sit on this evidence if I hadn't called round?" demanded Bill furiously. "We'll need to pull Deborah and Kelvin in again. And what of this Irish business? There was a bomb went off in the High Street here two years ago and a child was killed. I thought I had heard Jeffrey's name before. Two Irishmen were reported to have been staying in his flat the night before the bombing. He denied the whole thing and we had no evidence to hold him. But this time he's really going to sweat."

"We were going to phone you this evening," said James. "It's no use being angry with us, Bill, and telling us to keep out of it. You'd never have found all this out without our help. How did you find us?"

"Sir Charles told me where you were. He appeared to think that the hiring of you showed him to be innocent. I'd better get down to police headquarters right away, and you pair are coming with me!"

Later that evening Jeffrey Benson was returning from the Grapes. As he turned the corner of the street where he lived, he saw two men standing and looking up at his block of flats. There was something familiar about them, about the grey suits and grey faces. He recognized one of them. It was the man who had questioned him after the bombing. The man from MI5. He walked quickly away and went to a phone box. He took a small notebook out of his pocket and found a number and dialled. When a voice answered, he said, "Benson here, Dembley. They're waiting to question me again about that business two years ago."

"Then do what you did two years ago and keep your mouth shut," said the voice.

"But they'll keep me in for days and grill me," said Jeffrey, his voice sounding weak and frightened and not at all like his usual robust tones.

"You know what to do." The voice was cold. "Keep your mouth shut or we'll shut it for you."

"If that's all the help you are," shouted Jeffrey, "I've a good mind to tell them the lot and ask for protection."

"Just remember, there's no protection from us," said the voice.

Jeffrey walked out into a shifting world full of death and violence. For the first time in years, he thought of his mother. Like a lost child, he walked back to his street and approached the two men. "Looking for me?" he said.

Deborah had all her clothes spread out on the bed when the police came for her. She had been trying to think what to wear on Saturday. She had studied society magazines, but all they showed were pictures of people at balls and parties. They did not show any pictures of people at a country-house dinner.

And when they started to question her about that Saturday, she was terrified that they might arrest her and that she might never get to Barfield House for dinner.

116

* * *

Bill Wong called on Agatha and James on the following morning. He looked weary.

"We can't hold Deborah," he said. "She said she had started to drive out in the hope of stopping Jessica making a scene, but then had turned back to Dembley before she got to the estate. She's stuck to her story, although we questioned her over and over again. She said she turned back because she was frightened of Jessica, then she said she had lied to us because she was frightened of being accused of the murder.

"Kelvin has admitted to the row with Jessica. After intensive questioning it appears that he was so ashamed of his inability to lay her that he lied to us. Believe that if you want. Peter and Terry said they had volunteered for the extra work at the restaurant and changed shifts with two of the other waiters because no one was going out on that Saturday walk but Jessica. Now we get to Benson.

"He did house two Irishmen the night before the bombing. He swears blind he didn't know what they were going to do, that is if they did it. He's so terrified, he's told us all he knows and it's not much. We traced a phone number he gave us, but when we got there the four men who had been living in this house in Stratford had packed up and disappeared. They must have known he would sing. False names, rent paid cash, no contact with the neighbours. The usual dead end."

"I suppose he's under protective custody," said James.

"Not worth it. He's just one of those naïve liberals who get sucked in. He'll never hear from them again, and more's the pity. But that's all MI5's pigeon. We're still working on the murder."

117

"I suppose the walk on Saturday is off," said Agatha.

"Oh, no, you may as well go along and keep your ears open. I can't stop you. But go carefully. Sir Charles is still under suspicion, but it could well be one of your rambling companions. Make sure they don't suspect you. Jeffrey talks to you about Ireland in a pub, James, and the next day MI5 comes calling. He might put two and two together."

When he had left, James and Agatha looked at each other for a long moment. "I think you had better go home, Agatha," said James finally. "I don't like this."

But all in that moment the idea of giving up her precious role of Mrs. Lacey was more frightening to Agatha than the idea of being murdered.

"I've got you to protect me," she said. "We haven't even had any breakfast. I'll make it."

She hummed to herself in the kitchen as she prepared a cheese omelette for both of them, so engrossed in her wifely role that she quite forgot that she had never really made an omelette.

James came into the kitchen in time to smell burning cheese and swipe the pan off the stove. "Go and sit down, Agatha," he said in a kindly voice. "You're obviously too worried to cook."

And so Agatha had all the humiliation of sitting there feeling useless while James whipped up two light cheese omelettes. He doesn't need a wife, mourned Agatha. If the road to a man's heart is through his stomach, then I haven't got a hope in hell.

"What about Mary Trapp?" asked James.

"Oh, her? Maybe we'll talk to her on the walk," said Agatha. "I mean, it'll begin to look odd if we call on another one of them."

"We didn't exactly call on Deborah or Kelvin," James pointed out. "Still, maybe you're right. We'll have a day off. Tell you what, we'll go to the movies and forget about the whole thing."

Agatha had quite decided the pursuit of James was hopeless and was so quiet and subdued for the rest of that day and evening that James enjoyed her company immensely. And that night he didn't even bother to put a chair under the handle of his bedroom door.

It was a subdued group of ramblers who set out from the Grapes that Saturday. Agatha was still without any romantic hopes and was wearing the sneakers recommended by Alice. She felt they made her feet look enormous, but what did it all matter anyway? There was nothing to look forward to now at her age but an early grave.

Jeffrey Benson was suffering from total loss of ego. When he remembered the way he had cringed before his interrogators, he felt like bursting into tears. Then, when he had begged them for protection and they had told him in an almost fatherly way that he was of no account to anyone, he was just one of the saps the IRA had used, he had felt totally demoralized.

It was obvious that Alice and Gemma had had some sort of row because Gemma, wearing a brief pair of shorts and unsuitable, thin sandals, was talking animatedly to Mary Trapp while Alice lumbered behind, scowling. Peter and Terry were whispering together. James wondered how soon it would be before the ramblers connected him and Agatha with the sudden renewal of police interest and how the police had come by the new information. The one thing, he thought, that might save himself and Agatha from discovery was the walkers' lack of interest in anything other than their own immediate affairs. He looked down at Agatha, who was glooming along beside him, and decided it was time they reinforced the marital couple bit and said sharply to her, "What's the matter with you, dear? You look as if you've lost your last penny."

"Oh, shut up, pillock," snapped Agatha, correctly guessing what he was up to and glad of a way to release her pent-up frustrations. "It's a wonder you didn't ask that little tart from the library along."

"How dare you speak to me like that," said James. "Jeffrey's right. You need a punch in the mouth."

"What's that?" Mary Trapp swung round. "How dare you advocate violence against women, Jeffrey!"

"Ah'm sick o' this bickering," said Kelvin. He looked stonily at Agatha and James. "You two should keep your quarrels out o' public. There's nothing mair sickening than a marital row."

"How would *you* know, Kelvin," jeered Alice. "You can't even get a girl-friend."

Kelvin stood stock-still, his face flaming. "Ah'm sick o' the lot of ye. Ah'm going home."

"Now, then," said Peter. "Birds in their little nests agree. Are we out for a nice walk, or aren't we?"

They all walked on in silence. But as they reached the outskirts of Dembley, rusting recession-hit factories on either side of them, the grey clouds above parted and the sun shone down. Spirits began to lift. Gemma began to sing "One Man Went to Mow," and they all joined in.

By the time they reached the edge of the land across which they were to walk, they were all in a fairly good mood.

They consulted the map and the old book Jeffrey had found. "There should be signs," said Jeffrey. "But this is the way. Let's go."

They all climbed over a stile and along the edge of one field, but then they came up against a padlocked gate. Leaning on the other side of the gate was a large, brutal-looking man with a shotgun.

"Get off my land," he shouted. "Poxy ramblers. I'd shoot the lot of you."

"Who are you?" demanded Jeffrey, moving to the front of the group.

"My name is Harry Ratcliffe," said the farmer, "and you're on my land."

"You've got no right to order us off," said Jeffrey wrathfully. He brandished the map. "This is a legitimate right of way."

"Ah, to hell with you," said Ratcliffe. "Left-wing buggers. Why don't you go and get a job and cut your hair?"

Jeffrey could not bear one more humiliation. He thrust the map into Agatha's hands, vaulted over the gate and aimed a punch at the farmer. The farmer blocked his arm and swung his fist, which landed with a smack on Jeffrey's nose. "Let that be a lesson to you," shouted Ratcliffe. "I'm going for my dogs."

He strode off. James climbed over the gate and knelt beside Jeffrey. He mopped at the blood with his handkerchief and felt gingerly along the bridge of Jeffrey's nose. "You're lucky," he said. "Nothing broken. We'd best get you back before he turns the dogs on us. You'll feel better after a drink and then we'll go to the police." The injured Jeffrey was tenderly helped back over the gate. Fussing over him, they led their injured leader from the field.

121

They have a point, thought Agatha in surprise; some of these landowners are right bastards. She almost forgot about the murder. The attack on Jeffrey had drawn them all together wonderfully. By the time they were seated in the Grapes, the old Agatha had surfaced and was explaining how she would consult a lawyer and make sure the right of way was opened up.

Jeffrey, recovered after James had bought him two double brandies, said he did not want to go to the police, but he was grateful to Agatha for volunteering to make life hot for Ratcliffe. They all proceeded to drink quite a lot and everything was going merrily until Deborah was overheard asking Agatha what she should wear to dinner at Barfield House.

Mary Trapp rounded on her. "Never tell me you're going there! That's the enemy."

Deborah blushed painfully. "Sir Charles is all right," she said defensively. "He's not like Ratcliffe!"

"You are betraying your class," said Alice ponderously.

"Wear a pretty blouse and skirt," said James, addressing Deborah.

She looked at him in surprise. "But I bought a black velvet dinner gown from the thrift shop."

"Too overdressed," said James. "When in doubt, dress down, not up."

"You never were one of us, Deborah," said Jeffrey. "Trust you to go over to the other side."

Deborah did not say anything. She simply walked out of the pub. She was not going to let anything take the gloss off the forthcoming evening.

They watched her go and then fell to berating Ratcliffe

over again until cheerfulness was restored.

James and Agatha walked companionably home. "We'll get changed and go out for dinner," said James, and all Agatha's hopes flooded back into her tipsy brain and she startled James by accompanying him out to a hotel dining-room in a short black dress with a very low neckline indeed, very high heels and very much make-up.

It was a good thing, thought James, that he had not advised Agatha to dress down. Dressing down for the evening was obviously a foreign idea to Agatha Raisin!

SEVEN

†

DEBORAH drove out to Barfield House wearing the black velvet dinner gown. She had consulted the buyer in Dembley's most expensive dress shop and the buyer had said a dinner gown was de rigueur. The stultifying gentility of the buyer had impressed Deborah no end.

She was also clutching a silver sequinned evening bag.

Deborah was unlucky. It could easily have been formal dress and then her dinner gown, although a bit over the top for a young woman and more suitable for a dowager, would have fitted in with the scenery, but as the guests were simply some old friends Sir Charles had staying for the weekend, the dress was informal. She found that out as soon as she entered the drawing-room. Certainly the men were wearing collar and tie, but the women were in summer dresses. Deborah stood awkwardly in the doorway, feeling like a child widow.

Sir Charles sailed up and greeted her with a kiss on the cheek. "You're looking very slinky," he said, and just when

Deborah was beginning to feel better, he added, "Like that woman in the Addams Family."

Although his aunt should have introduced Deborah all round, as she acted as hostess for Sir Charles, Mrs. Tassy had not even looked up when Deborah entered, so Sir Charles did the honours. There were a Colonel and Mrs. Devereaux and their daughter, Sarah. Then a thin young man called Peter Hailey and his friend, small, chubby, and noisy, a Henry Barr-Derrington; and a heavy-set, brooding type of girl, Arabella Tierney. They all stared at Deborah when she was introduced. She said to each, "Pleased to meet you." Deborah would normally have said, "Pleased ter meet you," but she had been refining her accent.

It was not that anyone was precisely rude to her but more slightly surprised and then dismissive. That was it. She felt she had been summed up and dismissed. She thought she heard Henry murmur, "That must be Charles's latest aberration," but decided, as she had done in the past, that nervousness was making her hear insults that had never existed.

Mrs. Tassy then bore down on Deborah with the weary air of one recollecting her duties. "My dear child," she said, "such a *warm* frock. Aren't you too warm in that?"

"No, thank you, I'm fine," said Deborah, catching a malicious smile on the face of Gustav.

Gustav announced dinner. Deborah was relieved to learn she was sitting next to Sir Charles.

The table looked pretty with candles and flowers, and as the meal progressed, Deborah could not help noticing that it was a much simpler affair than the heavy lunch that had been inflicted on her when she came with Agatha. But, oh, she wished she had not come. They were all such dreadful snobs . . .

And then conversation turned to the murder and Sir Charles said that Deborah was one of the Dembley Walkers and Deborah immediately found herself the focus of attention. She was asked to tell them all about it. She did so, at first shyly, but then gaining confidence from their rapt attention, and when she finished up with a description of that day's walk and the confrontation with farmer Ratcliffe, she had the table's sympathy.

"That man is a boor," said the colonel roundly. "It's a pity your friend, Jeffrey, didn't manage to punch *him.*" And so the conversation went on about the iniquities of Ratcliffe until Mrs. Tassy rose to indicate the ladies should follow her to the drawing-room.

In the drawing-room Mrs. Devereaux sat down next to Deborah and asked her what subject she taught, and having learned it was physics asked her advice about helping a young nephew who was deficient in the subject, and that took up the time until the men joined them.

Deborah found that, by ignoring the very presence of Gustav, she was able to relax. Everyone was nice, after all. She became elated and quite pretty and when Peter and Henry began to tease her and flirt with her, she positively glowed.

When the evening finished and Sir Charles kissed her warmly on the cheek, she drove off feeling that no drug in the world could possibly give her the high she was on.

Later, Gustav stacked glasses in the dishwasher. Mrs. Pretty, hired from the village to cook for the evening, was sitting at the kitchen table drinking a glass of port. "So who's this girl Sir Charles has got?" she asked.

"How did you hear about her?" asked Gustav.

"People talk. They were seen together in Burger King. Is he serious about her? Will he marry her?"

"Over her dead body," said Gustav, and the cook laughed.

At one in the morning, Jeffrey heard a knock at his door. He had been watching a late movie and so had not gone to bed. At first he wondered whether it might be the police again and if he could pretend to be asleep, but as the knocking increased in force, he decided he had better answer it.

He opened the door. "Oh, it's you," he said, his voice light with relief. "Come in. I thought it was the police."

Agatha awoke to the sound of police sirens. She ran out of her bedroom and looked down from the kitchen window, which overlooked Sheep Street. Another police car raced past underneath.

James awoke with a start and stared at the white, mask-like face of Agatha Raisin looking down at him. She had forgotten all about the face pack she had put on before going to bed.

"What is it?"

"Police cars, lots of them, tearing out of Dembley," said Agatha. "Something's happened."

"May have nothing to do with our ramblers," said James sleepily.

Agatha tugged impatiently at his pyjama jacket. "Oh, come on, James. I feel it's something to do with our lot. Hurry!"

James grumbled but nonetheless got ready with such speed that he was down in the car and waiting for Agatha when she ran down to the street. "You've got little bits of face mask still about your ears," he said, and that miserable thought preoccupied Agatha as they drove out of Dembley, with her squinting into a compact mirror and scrubbing at the white clay with a handkerchief.

They were automatically heading for the Barfield estate when, across the fields in the light of the rising sun, they saw in the distance a little cluster of flashing blue lights.

"Ratcliffe's land," said James. They drove on in silence.

James stopped near the stile they had climbed over the day before, parking behind the police cars. A group of uniformed and plainclothes men were over by the gate where Jeffrey had had his fight with Ratcliffe.

As they walked up to the group, a policeman detached himself and ran towards them, holding up his hand and shouting, "Stay back!"

But then Bill Wong appeared and waved them forward. "What are you two doing here?" he demanded sharply.

"We heard the police cars and followed. What's happened?" asked Agatha, all the time praying: Don't let it be Deborah. If it's Deborah, I've failed.

"It's Jeffrey Benson," said Bill. "He's dead."

"Shot?" asked James. "Did Ratcliffe shoot him?"

"Ratcliffe's over there. What's this about Ratcliffe?"

James told him about the fight the day before. "We'll be questioning Ratcliffe," said Bill grimly. "He's the one who found the body. But at the moment it looks like an accident. Jeffrey was cutting the padlock on the gate, or that's what it looks like, when he fell and struck his head on a rock. But we'll know more after the pathologist gets a look at the body. We'll need a full statement from both of you and the other walkers."

"Do you think if he was murdered that it might be the IRA?" asked James.

"Hardly think so. A bullet in the back of the head is more their style. Or such an insignificant cog as Jeffrey was would get knee-capped at the most."

"Can we have a look?" asked Agatha. "We may be able to notice something that's different to yesterday."

"Wait there," commanded Bill. He went over and talked to his superiors. Several heads swivelled in their direction and then they were called forward. The crowd of men parted to let them through.

Jeffrey Benson lay sprawled on the ground below the gate. Beside him lay a huge pair of wire-cutters. On the other side of him lay a sharp rock.

"That rock wasn't there before," said Agatha.

"Are you sure?" demanded Bill.

"I think she's right," said James slowly. "It was such a violent scene that everything in the immediate vicinity became etched on our minds."

One of the forensic men in white overalls was called forward. He put a long steel implement under the rock and raised it gently. "Dry underneath," he said. "It certainly hasn't been here long."

"So," said Wilkes, speaking for the first time, "although at first sight it looks as if he was climbing over the gate, fell off, and broke his neck, it seems as if actually someone could have struck him a blow on the head with that rock. You pair had better get home and leave things to us. We'll see you later for a statement."

Agatha was led off by James. When they reached the stile, her teeth began to chatter and she stumbled as she was getting over. He had climbed over first. He reached up strong arms and lifted her down. It was one of the scenes Agatha had played out in her mind when she had dreamt of them rambling together, but now all she could do was wish she had never seen that dead body. She knew that it would haunt her dreams.

James fussed over her when they got home, making her drink a cup of hot sweet tea, take a couple of aspirin, and go back to bed.

She lay for a long time shivering, twisting and turning before she finally fell asleep.

The Dembley Walkers met in the Grapes the following evening at six because Peter and Terry were on duty at the restaurant at seven. Agatha and James were there, having been telephoned by a frantic Deborah, screaming that they were all going to be murdered, and what was Agatha *doing* about it?

James looked around the quiet and subdued group and said, "Where's Mary Trapp?"

"Helping the police with their inquiries," said Kelvin gloomily.

"Why?"

"Her neighbours said they heard her going out during the night. She's got a dotty dog lover living next door," said Peter. "Dog decides it wants walkies at two in the morning. Neighbour sees Mary all kitted out in her boots and shorts turning the corner of the street."

"Mary couldn't have done it, could she?" asked Agatha, thinking uneasily that they had not yet checked up on her.

"We were just talking about that before you came in," said Deborah. "None of us really knows anything about Mary, really. She and Jessica were close. But then Jessica was close to all of us." She began to cry. "I can't stand this."

"I suppose we all had alibis for last night?" said James.

He looked round the group. There was a gloomy shaking of heads. The murder had taken place during the night and all of them claimed to have been in their beds.

"I think they're still questioning Ratcliffe. He was once in prison for beating up a man in a pub," said Kelvin. "Mark ma words, this one had naethin' to dae with Jessica's murder. Jeffrey went out during the night wi' thae wire-cutters, Ratcliffe saw him, picked up thon rock and shied it at him and Jeffrey fell down dead."

"So it wasn't an accident?" asked Agatha.

"No," said Kelvin. "They're treating it as murder."

The door opened and Bill Wong came in, followed by a policeman and policewoman. He came up to their table. "Alice Dewhurst," he said, "we want you to accompany us to the station."

"Why?" demanded Alice, turning a muddy colour.

"Just a few questions. Come along."

"What's that all about?" they asked Gemma.

She shrugged. "I don't know, I'm sure."

"Was Alice with you all night?" asked Peter.

Again that shrug. "Don't ask me. I took one of them barbiturates and was dead to the world until she brought my tea in the morning."

"Don't worry, sweetie," said Terry. "You know Alice could never have done it."

"I dunno," said Gemma to their surprise. "Got ever such a nasty temper."

"But why on earth would she want to biff Jeffrey?" asked Agatha.

"Maybe because she thought he killed Jessica," said Gemma, scooping up a handful of peanuts from a bowl on the table.

"Not very loyal, are we, darling?" commented Terry.

"Actually I'm a bit tired of Alice," said Gemma, looking earnestly round at them. "She gets on my tits."

"Oh, we all knew *that,* sweetie," said Peter and nudged Terry and sniggered.

Peter turned his attention to James and Agatha. "And just what were our loving couple doing last night?"

"What do you think?" asked James.

"Oh, don't pull that one. I should have thought romance went down the plug hole for you pair a million years ago." Peter sounded suddenly waspish.

"You'd better watch out, you dismal little twit, or I'll biff *you,*" said Agatha. "Shouldn't you and your fairy friend here be off to that slum of a restaurant to serve up another dose of salmonella to your customers?"

"Nasty, nasty," chided Peter, quite unfazed. "Come on, Terry. Duty calls."

The party broke up with their going. James and Agatha went back to their flat.

"Well," said James gloomily, "I haven't a clue. What about you?"

Agatha shook her head. "As far as I'm concerned, any

133

of them could have done it. I can't look at them objectively any more. I'm beginning to dislike the lot of them."

"Let's have a drink and think about dinner. What do you want?"

"Gin and tonic, please. Oh, there's someone at the door."

James put down the gin bottle and went to answer it. He hoped it wasn't one of the walkers. He felt he had had enough of them for one day.

But it was Bill Wong, who said, "May I come in? I have some news that might interest you."

He refused a drink. "Is it about Alice?" asked Agatha.

He nodded. "We've been digging into the past life of all the suspects. We got some old newsreel film of the Greenham Common women. One report, trying to prove they were all noisy slags, had interesting footage of Alice and Jessica, a younger Alice and Jessica, having a stand-up fight. Now Alice said in her statement that she did not know Jessica before Jessica came to Dembley, so why did she lie?"

"And what does she say?" asked James.

"She says she had forgotten all about it, that she always thought there was something familiar about Jessica. She's still lying, but we can't get her to say anything else. Now if Jeffrey knew anything about her and Alice, Alice might have decided to shut him up. She could have called on him and suggested it would be a great idea to get even with Ratcliffe by cutting the padlock on that gate."

"Were the wire-cutters hers?" asked Agatha.

"No luck there. Jeffrey had bought them himself six weeks ago to get even with another landowner who had padlocked and chained a gate over a right of way. You've been with these people. You were on that walk. There must be one of them who struck you as being capable of murder."

James looked at Agatha, and Agatha looked at James. Both shook their heads.

"These murders have twisted up my mind so much that I look at them and think any of them could have done it," said James.

Bill sighed. "Normally I would be telling you pair to go home and forget about all this, but I keep hoping that in your amateur way you might hit on something."

"What about forensic evidence?" asked Agatha. "Footprints, fingerprints?"

"Can't get anything off that rock, and the ground was bone-dry and hard. Jeffrey's car was found nearby. They're going over that inch by inch. It'll take some time for all the fibres, if there are any, to be analysed and traced. I'm tired. Pray for just one break before anyone else gets murdered!"

When Bill had left, James said, "What about going back to Carsely and putting everything we've got on the word processor and then see if we can hit on something."

"I may as well see my cats," said Agatha. "Should I bring them back with me?"

"If you like," he said moodily. "But I don't think there's any point in us staying here much longer."

Agatha glanced round the flat which had become their home for such a brief period. All her dreams of romance with James had faded away. They somehow seemed to have settled down to living together like two old bachelors.

Once back at Carsely, she fed and petted her cats, although deciding not to take them to Dembley with her, before going next door and joining James at the word processor. But before he had started typing out the first list of names, his doorbell went and he soon returned, followed by Mrs. Mason.

"I saw your car outside," she said to Agatha. "How are things going?"

"Very slowly," said Agatha.

"I'm worried about poor little Deborah," said Mrs. Mason, heaving her corseted bulk into a chair. "This other murder—I saw it on the six-o'clock news—must be frightening her to death." She preened slightly. "Thank goodness she has Sir Charles to look after her. Do you know she went to Barfield House for dinner last night?"

"She said something about that," remarked Agatha. "She was asking what to wear. How did that go? I forgot to ask her."

"Oh, she said it was wonderful and his friends were ever so nice to her." Mrs. Mason patted her grey permed hair. "I think we might have a Lady in the family soon."

"I shouldn't think so," said James idly, staring at the word processor. He wondered what Mrs. Mason would say if she ever knew her beloved niece had been having a lesbian affair with Jessica.

Mrs. Mason bristled. "Don't you think my Deborah good enough?"

"What?" James swung round. "No, no, I was just thinking one invitation to a dinner party does not make a marriage."

"But Deborah says he's ever so keen on her. She's a bright girl. She was the first in our family ever to go to university. My poor sister, Janice, had ever such a bad time with that husband of hers. Bad lot, he was. Poor little thing.

136

So clever and pretty. Do see if you can find out who's doing these dreadful killings."

She refused an offer of tea and left. James returned to typing out lists of names, one on each page. Then he and Agatha began to put down what they knew of each one.

"Do you know," said Agatha, stifling a yawn, "I still think any of them could have done it. They're not a very nice crowd."

"You'd better get some sleep."

"And something to eat," said Agatha.

"Tell you what, as we're leaving for Dembley in the morning, fetch your case along here. I'll fix us an omelette or something and you can sleep in my spare room." His eyes were kind, and Agatha knew that he was concerned for her because of her shock over the murder.

"Thank you," she said quietly.

She went back and collected a suitcaseful of clean clothes, not really bothering much what she put in this time. The idea of having supper with James and sleeping under his roof in Carsely would have sent her into Seventh Heaven only a short time ago. But the last murder had brought her face to face with the brutal realities of life. She was a middle-aged woman with a wrinkled upper lip who should accept that fact and stop being silly.

It was just as well she did not know that James was beginning to enjoy her company as never before. While she was in her own cottage, packing, he put clean sheets on the spare-room bed and went to rummage through the kitchen cupboards to find something for supper. He reflected that having someone around gave structure to his days, and when a weary Agatha returned on his doorstep, he took her suitcase from her and carried it upstairs without feeling in the slightest bit wary of her.

Over a supper of ham omelette and a bottle of chilled white wine, he talked idly about his army days and then, when she had finished eating, went upstairs to the bathroom and ran a bath for her and told her gently to get ready for bed.

"Maybe we'll have a bit of luck if we try again, Agatha," he said. "Have a bath and a good night's sleep and if you have any bad dreams, just wake me up."

"Thank you, James," said Agatha humbly. She stood on tiptoe and kissed him on the cheek and went upstairs.

James whistled to himself as he did the dishes.

"Will that be all?" Gustav asked Sir Charles.

"Yes, thank you," said Sir Charles vaguely from behind his newspaper. Then, as Gustav was leaving the room, he lowered it and said, "Wait a bit. There is something. Did Aunt get off to London all right?"

"Yes, I took her to the station. The train was on time for once."

"Good, good. I want you to take the day off tomorrow, Gustav."

"Why?"

"Do you have to know? Well, I have invited Miss Camden round for lunch and I don't want you glooming about the place."

"Meaning you're going to screw her."

"Who I screw or don't screw is entirely my business, Gustav. Just leave out something for a simple lunch and bugger off. And don't try to intimidate her this time with forty courses and twenty canteens of cutlery. Cold pie, potato salad, something like that. Decent bottle of wine. We'll eat in the kitchen. Now go away."

Gustav stood his ground. "You should stick to your own type."

"You're a dreadful snob."

"Not me. Some farmer's daughter would be suitable, even some farm labourer's daughter. And talking of farm labourers, did you sack Noakes yet?"

"Can't see any reason to. He told the police what he saw. Help's hard to come by these days. Can't do it all by machine."

"Wish you could do Deborah Camden by machine, sir. You might catch something."

"Oh, get out, you dirty-minded bugger."

"Don't say I didn't warn you," was Gustav's parting shot. "That one's creepy."

James and Agatha decided next day, after unpacking their bags, to go to the Copper Kitchen for lunch, for, as James pointed out, that gossipy pair, Peter and Terry, might let another few gems of information fall.

They both ordered fish and chips, thinking that the chef at the Copper Kitchen might be able to cook something so undemanding, but the fish proved to be of the breaded kind, frozen in bulk and sold to such restaurants. It was amazingly tasteless, as were the chips; even the tartar sauce had no taste at all.

"Thought the others might be in," said Peter, stopping by their table. "Founder's day at the school, so they're on holiday."

"I didn't think comprehensive schools had founders," commented Agatha. "I thought they were founded by the local council."

"Well, this one has. So what are the leisured classes doing today?"

James thought quickly. He could hardly say, "Investigating this case to find out if one of you did it."

Instead he said, "We might run over to Stratford and see if we can get tickets for this evening. Ages since I've seen a Shakespeare play."

"Oh, you could run a little errand for me, then," said Peter. "Deborah's over at her mother's. I borrowed a kettle from her, she had a spare, and she keeps nagging me and I always forget to give it back. I've got it here."

"Can't you just give it to her next time you see her?" asked James.

"I *could,* sweetie, but then I'd forget again. Now, if you took it, it would be your responsibility."

"All right," said James. "Give us the mother's address."

Peter went off and returned with an electric kettle and a slip of paper with Mrs. Camden's address. "It's a council estate," said Peter. "Far side of Stratford from here." James made a neat note of the directions.

"Do we want to get to Stratford? Dreary dump," said Agatha, as they got in the car.

"We're supposed to be investigating. If Deborah's there, she might be able to tell us something more."

As they drove off in the direction of Stratford, Agatha felt relief that she no longer seemed to be obsessed with James, that in a way she had grown up and was content with friendship.

140

She remembered a typist called Fran she had once employed at her PR agency. Fran had mooned and talked and mooned and talked about a man she fancied who worked for another PR firm. At last Agatha and the rest had pointed out that it was the twentieth century and there was nothing to stop her phoning the man up and asking him out for a drink. They had all stood over her until she had picked up the phone and done just that. He said he would meet her for a drink on the Friday evening after work.

They told her what to wear right down to the underwear and scent. They told her what to talk about and how to behave and then sent her off on Friday.

On Monday morning Agatha stopped by Fran's desk and asked, "How did it go?"

"I didn't meet him," said Fran.

"What!" exclaimed Agatha. "Didn't he show?"

She remembered Fran's little resigned sigh and how she had said, "I went right up to the door of the pub and looked in and he was there at the bar, waiting. So I turned and walked away. You see, I'd dreamt and dreamt about him for so long that I realized he could not possibly live up to my dreams and expectations. I'm not into reality."

But I am . . . now, thought Agatha, and it feels good.

After several mistakes, they found Mrs. Camden's address. It was a terraced council house. The garden was weedy, scraggly flower-beds surrounding a balding lawn. The gate sagged on its hinges.

The house had a neglected, deserted air, and they were almost surprised when they heard someone approaching on the other side of the door to answer their knock.

The woman who opened the door was somehow recognizable as Deborah's mother. She had the same skinny

141

bleached look, but her shoulders were stooped and the only colour about her was in her work-reddened hands.

"We are friends of Deborah's," said Agatha. "Is she here? It is Mrs. Camden?"

"Yes, come in. Deborah's not here, but I was just about to put the kettle on."

"We've got a kettle of Deborah's here," said James, brandishing it. "Should we leave it with you?"

"I'll take it. She might be over this evening." A smile transformed Mrs. Camden's thin white face. "She'll be anxious to tell me the news."

"Oh, about the murder," remarked Agatha. She led them into a small living-room. It contained a few battered chairs, a sofa, and a chipped table. There were no books or pictures, only a television set in the corner flickering away. Mrs. Camden switched it off. "Make yourselves comfortable," she said. "I'll get the tea."

Agatha introduced them both to her as Mr. and Mrs. Lacey, getting the usual little thrill when she mentioned the names. Then she and James sat down side by side on the sofa. "It's bleak," muttered James.

"She doesn't seem to be working," whispered Agatha. "I wonder if Deborah gives her any money."

The miserable room silenced them. The wind had risen outside. A piece of newspaper blew against the window panes, staring at them like a face, and then blew away.

Mrs. Camden returned with a tray on which were china cups decorated with roses, a teapot, milk, sugar, and a plate of biscuits.

After tea was poured, Agatha said sympathetically, "You must be very worried about your daughter."

"Oh, because of these dreadful murders? But Deborah

has always been the strong one. Thank goodness. And now she's going to be Lady Fraith."

They both stared at her.

"Are you sure?" asked James.

"Yes, she's gone over there today and she knows he's going to pop the question."

"Are you sure she isn't imagining things?" asked James cautiously.

"Oh, no," said Mrs. Camden with supreme confidence. "Deborah always knows what's what. Mind you, it was a bit of a blow when she said that me and Mark and Bill— that's her brothers—couldn't come to the wedding."

Agatha looked at her in a dazed way. "Why not?"

"It wouldn't be fitting. I mean, we're not of Sir Charles's class."

"Neither is Deborah," pointed out James.

"But she's made herself that way," said Mrs. Camden. "I'm that proud of her. She was always the hope of the family."

"Are you working?" asked Agatha. It seemed later an odd thing to ask, but there was something about Mrs. Camden's stooped figure which seemed to suggest years of drudgery.

"I have my cleaning jobs," she said. "And then I work in the supermarket at weekends."

"Deborah must be able to help you out a bit," said James.

"She can't."

"Why not?" asked Agatha.

"She needs all her money to keep up the right appearance. She's amazing. Even when she was little, she would say, 'Mum, I'm going to the university and I'm going to be a teacher.' And so she did. So when she said to me, 'I'm going to marry Sir Charles Fraith and live in that big house,' I knew she meant it."

"And what of your sons?" asked Agatha.

She sighed. "They take after their father. They're both in a council flat in Stratford, on the dole, but at least they're not under my feet."

"Do you know where your husband is?" asked Agatha.

She shook her head. "Don't want to know, either. He was a violent man. I'm not complaining. Deborah's my whole life. Let me show you something." She stood up and walked from the room and they followed her.

She pushed open a door. "This was Deborah's room." She stood aside to let them pass.

James and Agatha stood shoulder to shoulder and looked in awe at the bedroom. It was a sort of shrine. The bed had a pretty coverlet and was covered with dolls and stuffed animals. The walls were covered with photographs of Deborah. Deborah as a baby, as a toddler, at school, at university. There were long low bookshelves containing books, the shells of Deborah's life, from the brightly coloured children's books right through to the works of Marx.

The wind moaned louder and the branches of a dead tree tapped against the window.

"Very impressive," said Agatha in a weak voice. They returned to the living-room which, after the bright bedroom, hit them afresh with its sad, shabby dullness.

Mrs. Camden sat down again with a sigh. "It was something to work for," she said. "You know, seeing Deborah had the best of everything."

"Surely you don't need to work so hard now?" suggested James.

"Well, girls always need something extra these days. She needed help getting her little car, and things like that. How did you come to meet my girl?"

"We are both retired," said James, "and we joined the Dembley Walkers, just after the murder."

"Good exercise," commented Mrs. Camden.

James looked at her in surprise. "You do not seem very frightened for the welfare of your daughter, considering there have now been two murders."

"Sir Charles will look after her," she said comfortably. "She says the first thing she's going to do as soon as they are married is get rid of that servant, Gustav. Is that his name?"

"She seems very sure of herself," was all Agatha could think of saying.

"Mmm." Mrs. Camden's face was again illuminated with that smile. "Although I won't be at the wedding, I'll read about it in the society magazines. Just think of that!"

"Deborah must have been upset at Jessica Tartinck's death," said James.

"What?" Mrs. Camden came out of her rosy dream. "Oh, that strapping big woman. But Deborah told me she was always getting people's backs up. I mean, it was bound to happen sooner or later."

Agatha stood up. She suddenly wanted to get away. She had never considered herself a particularly sensitive person, but she was now assailed with such a feeling of impending doom that she was desperate to get out of that shabby living-room.

"We must go," she said abruptly.

As if suffering from the same feelings, James leaped to his feet and held open the door for Agatha.

Once they were in the car, Agatha, who was driving, said, "Let's find somewhere quiet. I need to think."

She drove out of Stratford and parked in a lay-by and switched off the engine and looked blankly at the wind whipping through the trees at the side of the road.

"Why is it," she said in a thin voice, "that I feel I've just escaped from a madhouse?"

"Deborah appears to have been selfish from the day she was born, but the thing that frightens me is this wedding business. There's something else," said James. "It just occurred to me. There was something very hush-hush about Sir Charles's father's death. I remember someone telling me he died mad."

"What kind of mad?" asked Agatha. "I mean, no one ever says *mad* these days."

"Does it matter? For some reason Sir Charles has been leading Deborah into thinking he's going to marry her. I don't believe he means to for a moment."

Agatha stared at him. "And Deborah's there. Now. At Barfield House."

"Fast as you can, Agatha," said James. "I don't like this. I don't like this at all."

EIGHT

†

DEBORAH sailed up the drive to Barfield House in her little car. Her heart was light. Sir Charles had told her that Gustav had been given the day off and that his aunt was in London.

Sir Charles answered the door. He was wearing an old open-necked shirt and jeans, making her glad that she wasn't too "dressy." She was wearing a pink silk blouse from Marks & Spencer and a short navy acrylic skirt with a slit at the back and white sandals.

She approved of the kitchen, which was large and modern. So much more cheerful than the dark-panelled rooms of the rest of the house.

Sir Charles, as he opened a bottle of wine and listened to her prattling away about her teaching job, eyed her thoughtfully. He intended getting her into bed after lunch but was beginning to wonder how she would react. Her thinness and whiteness still excited him. He liked her shy little voice, so different from the robust tones of the girls he usually dated. Her neck was thin and fragile-looking. It looked as if it could almost be snapped like a flower stalk, he thought. He said, "Any news about Jeffrey's murder?"

Deborah shook her head. "They've been questioning and questioning all of us. They've still got Alice."

"The big one? Why her?"

"She knew Jessica ages ago and lied about it."

Sir Charles looked at her shrewdly. "If the police still have her in for questioning, how do you know that?"

"There's one of the teachers at the school whose sister works at police headquarters. She told me."

"Do you think Alice did it, then?"

"She could have done," said Deborah. "She's got ever such a bad temper."

As they ate, Sir Charles wondered how he was going to get around to proposing that they go upstairs to bed. Perhaps he should suggest they have coffee in the drawing-room and get down to work on the sofa first.

He really loves me, thought Deborah with a fast-beating heart. I can tell by the look in his eyes.

Conversation was flagging towards the end of the meal and then Deborah said, "Can I go and powder my nose?"

He saw his chance. "Come upstairs and use my bath-room."

He led the way upstairs and along a corridor and opened a door. Deborah glanced quickly about his bed-room. She was disappointed that there wasn't a four-poster bed but a modern one. The room, like the rest of the rooms in the house, was dark because of the tiny panes of the mullioned windows.

"In here," said Sir Charles, opening a door off the bedroom.

Deborah went in and closed the door behind her. Sir Charles jerked open the drawer of a bedside table to check that the packet of condoms he had bought was still there and that Gustav had not found them and taken them away, an act which would have been perfectly in keeping with Gustav's character.

There were shuffling noises from the bathroom. Deborah was taking a long time. The rising wind outside gave a cheerless moan. Sir Charles shivered. His lust was ebbing fast. It all began to seem silly.

And then the bathroom door opened and Deborah stood there. She was wearing nothing more than a brief bra, a suspender belt, and black stockings.

Sir Charles walked towards her, saying huskily, "Come to bed, Deborah."

"Is this as fast as you can go?" asked James.

"I'm going as fast as I can," wailed Agatha. "But that poxy tractor won't move, and I can't get past it." She pressed the horn and flashed her lights. The tractor driver raised two fingers. Just when Agatha was thinking she might drive straight into the back of him in a sheer fury, he turned off into a farm gate and Agatha roared past, relieving her feelings with another blast on the horn.

"But why would he kill Jeffrey?" she asked.

"He might have a thing about ramblers. If he's crazy like his father, he might not need a motive."

Agatha raced round a bend and screeched to a halt. A line of cars stretched out in front of her. She got out of the car and peered ahead. Some distance in front of the line of cars a truck was slewed across the road. A small mini was crushed in a ditch.

"Bugger, an accident," said Agatha, getting back into the car. She beat the steering wheel with her hands in sheer frustration. Then she saw to her right an open farm gate. She set off, swinging the wheel. The car lurched crazily over a field of wheat.

"What are you doing?" shouted James. "The farmer will kill us."

"I'll compensate him," yelled Agatha. "Barfield is over this way. I'm going as the crow flies." And with that the car plunged headlong into a ditch at the end of the field.

Agatha felt like bursting into tears. "Now what do we do?" she wailed.

James's face was grim and set. "We get out and ramble!"

Sir Charles and Deborah lay on their backs, immersed in their different thoughts. What a mistake, Sir Charles was thinking gloomily. That had been like making love to a corpse. Besides, she smelt like something off the burning-ghats of India. In the bathroom, Deborah had anointed her body with an aromatic oil from a new shop in Dembley called Planet Earth, which specialized in aromatherapy.

And then he was aware Deborah was speaking. "When we're married—and I hope you don't mind this, Charles dear—I would like to paint all that wood panelling white."

"Married?" croaked Sir Charles.

"Of course your aunt will need to find somewhere else to live. Can't have two women in one house. My mother says . . . my mother used to say, it never works. Isn't there a dower house or something?" asked Deborah with vague memories of Georgette Heyer novels.

Sir Charles swung his legs out of bed and began to

struggle into his clothes. "You should have a bath, darling," chided Deborah. She stretched and yawned. "Run one for me."

"Okay," said Sir Charles gloomily. He zipped up his trousers and padded on his bare feet into the bathroom and turned on the taps.

He turned round and let out a squawk of dismay. Deborah must have moved like lightning. She was standing behind him wearing his dressing-gown.

He turned away and stared down at the rushing water. "Look, Deborah," he said, "we've had a bit of a fling, that's all. I never said anything about marriage." He tried to laugh. "Not the marrying kind, me."

"But you've got to marry me!" Deborah sounded more surprised than angry.

"No, Deborah," he said firmly. "I am not marrying you or anyone. I said absolutely nothing to give you that impression. I would never have had sex with you if I thought you were going to jump to this mad conclusion."

"Mad?" Her voice was thin and brittle. "Mad?"

"We had a bit of fun, dear, let's leave it at that." He turned back to the bath. "Would you like some old-fashioned bath salts? Now, where did I put them?"

"Here, *dear!*" Deborah brought a glass jar of rose-scented bath salts down on his head.

Agatha's tights were ripped and she had pulled off the sweater she had been wearing over a blouse and thrown it away because she was sweating so much. She had a blister on one heel and a stitch in her side. James had taken her hand as they raced together through crops of golden oilseed rape and fields of blue flax flowers, wheat, and turnips.

"Are you sure we're going the right way?" shouted James.

"Yes," shouted back Agatha, who enjoyed studying ordnance survey maps as a pastime. But one bit of the countryside was beginning to look so much like another that she could hardly believe it when at last at some distance across the fields she saw the bulk of Barfield House.

She plunged gamely on, forgetting about the blister on her heel and the stitch in her side. Deborah was in danger. She, Agatha, the great detective, had been called in to help Deborah, and help Deborah she must.

Deborah turned off the bath taps and looked down at the unconscious Sir Charles Fraith as he lay on his own bathroom floor. The air around smelt of roses.

She sat down on a bathroom chair and stared bleakly in front of her. It had all been for nothing. All of it. And yet her mind felt quite cold and set. She knew what she had to do.

She dressed neatly and carefully and then went around and wiped every surface she might have touched, scrubbing and polishing, cocking her head occasionally in case there was the sound of an approaching car. Then she seized Sir Charles by the ankles and began to drag him out of the bathroom, out of the bedroom, slowly along the corridor and then, bump, bump, bump, down the stairs and then slid him easily across the polished floor of the hall, along the corridor at the end and, bump, bump, down the two steps to the kitchen.

She then set about cleaning up the kitchen, clearing and washing the remains of the meal, her mind carefully sorting things out. Gustav would tell the police she had been invited. But she had been incredibly lucky so far. It was Gustav's word against her own. All she had to do was to stick to her story. She pulled Sir Charles over to the oven and turned on the gas. She frowned. Wasn't there something about North Sea gas not doing the job the way the old coal gas used to? Perhaps she was worrying over too much. She heaved his head into the oven, then looked around. She picked up two dishcloths and got out various cleaning rags. She went out and shut the kitchen door behind her and stuffed the cloths and rags under the space at the bottom of the door.

She went into Sir Charles's study, where she remembered seeing a typewriter. All she had to do was find some documents with his signature on them, forge his signature to a typed suicide note, in which he also confessed to the murders of Jeffrey and Jessica. But a handwriting expert would no doubt find the signature to be a forgery. Oh, well, she thought on a sigh, she would just need to leave an unsigned note. It was such a pity about handwriting experts; without their interference it might have been possible to make out a will supposed to be from Sir Charles, leaving everything to her. Everything.

For one moment, her eyes filled with weak tears. All her dreams. Everything. She had imagined holding fêtes and garden parties at Barfield, with her in a wide shady straw hat greeting the guests, maybe making the opening speech. She blinked her tears away. She sat down at Sir Charles's desk and began to type.

Agatha and James ran up the drive of Barfield House. Behind them in the distance they could hear the wail of police sirens. "Something must have happened," panted Agatha.

"I think *we* might be what's happened," said James. "Angry farmers phoning in with reports about trespassers. God, this is beginning to seem ridiculous." He grabbed Agatha's arm, forcing her to stop. "We can't go bursting into Barfield House, shouting, 'We know you did it because your father was mad.'"

"Deborah's car's there," said Agatha stubbornly. "You can do what you like, but I'm just going to walk in and say I knocked and no one answered."

She heaved at the handle of the massive door and let out a sigh of relief when it swung open. James followed her into the hall. He was beginning to think the only person who was mad was Agatha. How on earth were they going to explain themselves?

And then Agatha said, "Gas. There's a smell of gas. Where the kitchen?"

"The smell seems to be coming from there," said James, pointing off the hall and down the corridor. They ran along and immediately saw the rags under the door. They pulled open the door. Agatha rushed across to the oven, turned off the gas, and flung open the kitchen windows.

"I'll call the police," said James.

Approaching sirens wailed from outside.

"They're here," said James. "I'll go and meet them. Oh, God, it was Deborah all the time, unless Gustav has murdered both of them."

He went back out, but as he was approaching the door, he heard the sound of a typewriter coming from the study. He pushed open the study door. Deborah was sitting typing, her back to him. He took off his belt and crept up behind her, then whipped it round her to pin her arms to her side.

The loud screams of invective that burst from Deborah's lips drowned out the sound of the sirens.

James and Agatha sat in the flat in Sheep Street that evening, sharing a bottle of wine and waiting for Bill Wong to call on them as he had promised. Both felt that it was unfair that the reason for the convenient police presence at Barfield House had been because both of them had been charged with trespass, some irate farmer reporting how two hooligans had driven their car right through his crop, dumped their car in the ditch, and taken off across the fields to trample down more crops on foot.

"Deborah! I just don't understand it," said Agatha, for seemingly the umpteenth time. "Oh, there's the doorbell. That must be Bill."

James rose and went to let him in. Bill looked weary. He accepted James's offer of a glass of wine, saying he was off duty, and then turned to Agatha. "How did you suss out it was Deborah?"

Agatha flashed James a little warning look and said airily, "Woman's intuition. But we'd rather hear all about it from you, Bill." She did not want to lose face by admitting to Bill Wong that they had thought the murderer was Sir Charles.

Bill shook his head in bewilderment. "She must be crazy. She told us the whole thing in this little-girl voice, on and on and on. She had always driven herself on to get away from her background, aided and abetted by her doting mother. The reason she had an affair with Jessica was not because Deborah is lesbian but, would you believe it, because she thought Jessica was 'good class.' Jessica had been to Oxford, you see. Deborah had adopted the politics of Jessica and her friends as a passport to a better society. I think it was on the fatal day Sir Charles invited her for tea that something in her snapped. Even over the first cup of tea, she saw a chance of becoming Lady Fraith. 'Jessica was in my way,' she kept saying over and over again. She was terrified Jessica might tell Sir Charles about that lesbian affair, terrified that Jessica would spoil her, Deborah's chances by creating a scene. Can I have some more wine?"

James filled his glass. Bill took a sip of wine and went on. "She was amazingly lucky. She drove to the Barfield estate. She said she wanted to catch up with Jessica before she did any damage. She found Jessica at the edge of that field. When she let out that she was keen on Sir Charles, how Jessica had laughed! It seems Jessica, once the gloves were off, was a middle-class snob of the worst kind. She sneered at Deborah for her accent, background, and clothes, said she hadn't a hope in hell, said she would let Sir Charles know about Deborah's lesbianism. Then Jessica started stamping her way across that field. Deborah saw the spade and saw red at the same time. She ran up behind Jessica, keeping in her tracks, and brought the spade down on her head. When she found Jessica was dead, she scraped and dug that shallow grave—when you think of all those plant roots, it must have taken manic strength—buried the body, wiped the shovel, and took off."

"But she asked Mrs. Mason for my help," cried Agatha. "Why would she do that?"

Bill looked rueful. "You're not going to like this. Evidently Mrs. Mason had given Deborah the impression that

156

you were an inept amateur, taking credit for police work, and so that by hiring you, she would look innocent and yet be in no danger of being found out."

"I will never speak to Mrs. Mason again," said Agatha wrathfully. "Old toad. I never liked her anyway."

Bill smiled at her and took up his story. "As I say, she was amazingly lucky. Her car had been seen on the road out of Dembley, but no one had actually seen her going into the estate. Then the waters were muddied by Sir Charles's lying about what he had been doing and by the others' lying as well.

"But why Jeffrey?" asked James.

"Ah, well, she had let slip in the pub that she was going to dinner at Barfield House. Jeffrey, who had got a bit tipsy after his confrontation with Ratcliffe, phoned her up just as she was leaving for Barfield House and asked her to come round, saying he was a better bet any day than Sir Charles. Deborah told him to get lost. He then told her, maliciously, that he had a good mind to tell Sir Charles about her affair with Jessica. Deborah said, still in that awful little voice, that she didn't take it really seriously until she was on her way back from the dinner at Barfield House. She decided to 'silence' him. So she changed and went round to his flat. She suggested they should get even with Ratcliffe. She and Jeffrey should drive out and cut the chain that held that padlocked gate and then both return to Jeffrey's flat for a bit of whoopee. So Jeffrey went like a lamb, cut the chain, and got struck on the head by Deborah, who had searched around while he was doing it and found that rock.

"She had somehow persuaded herself when Sir Charles asked her for that lunch he was all was set for marriage. When he told her he had no intention of marrying her, she

157

went right round the twist. That was why she was still working on that fake suicide note when you found her, James, even though she heard the police sirens outside. She was bewildered. All her life, she said, she had been driving towards the top. Do you know, in the beginning, getting to be a schoolteacher, for Deborah, was like an actor winning the Oscar. For a while, I think that was enough."

"It was the mad father who set us off to Barfield House," said James, and then stifled a yelp as Agatha kicked him. Agatha was determined that Bill should think they had guessed that Deborah was the one who had committed the murders.

"Oh, yes, Deborah's father," said Bill to Agatha's surprise. "Yes, we found he's in that prison for the criminally insane, Tadmartin. He'd murdered a woman he was living with, the one he left Mrs. Camden for."

"Did either Mrs. Camden or Deborah know this?" asked James.

"I don't think so," said Bill.

"Lots of madness in this," said James, drawing his legs out of Agatha's reach. "There was something in the back of my mind that Sir Charles's father died mad."

"No, he died drunk," said Bill. "Terrible old sot, he was. It's a pity you two are going to have to appear in court yourselves for trespass and damage to crops after all your hard work."

"Yes, I think you might have overlooked that," commented Agatha.

"Can't," said Bill. "The irate farmer won't let us."

"How's Sir Charles?" asked James.

"Lucky to be alive," said Bill. "He's in Dembley Central Hospital suffering from a bad concussion and cracked ribs. He got his ribs cracked when she dragged him down the stairs. She hit him on the head with a bottle of bath salts and then dragged him down the stairs to the kitchen. Well, I'd best be off. Thanks a lot, you two. We'd have got Deborah all right in the end. There was no way she could really cover up the murder of Sir Charles. We wouldn't have believed that suicide note for a moment. But it's thanks to you two that Sir Charles is alive. I suppose you'll be heading back to Carsely?"

"There's nothing to keep us here," said James. "I never want to see any of those walkers again."

When Bill had gone, Agatha said, "I suppose we ought to have something to eat. I don't feel like going out, do you?"

The doorbell sounded again. "Now, who can that be?" asked James. "I wish this door had a spyhole. If it's one of those ramblers, I'll swear I'll slam the door in their face."

He stepped back in surprise when he saw Gustav. The manservant entered. He handed James two bottles of old port. "The best in the cellars," he said. "Sir Charles has just recovered consciousness."

Gustav smiled directly at Agatha for the first time. "I understand from the police that Sir Charles would not be alive were it not for the pair of you. I am deeply grateful."

A gratified Agatha promptly forgot all her dislike of Gustav and begged him to sit down, but he shook his head. "My place is with Sir Charles. Do call and see him tomorrow. He will wish to thank you himself."

"He's quite human after all," said Agatha in surprise when Gustav had left. "Do we sample that port or do we save it for a special occasion?"

"I think this is a special occasion," said James with a

smile. "I'll look out some biscuits and cheese and perhaps that will do instead of dinner."

Agatha had, in the past, in the PR days, been offered and had drunk what had merely passed for vintage port. After James had decanted a bottle, she accepted a glass, amazed that with her depraved palate, educated through the years with gin and tonics and microwave meals, she should appreciate it so much. It went down like silk. It was also very heady and somehow it seemed to disappear very quickly, and it seemed only right to decant and sample the second bottle.

And then, as they mulled over the case, in increasingly tipsy accents, it suddenly struck James as terribly funny that Agatha had driven across that farmer's field. He began to laugh and soon Agatha was giggling helplessly and that was when James suddenly stopped laughing and took her face between his hands and kissed her on the lips. All the pent-up passion in Agatha rose to meet his lips and then his wandering hands, and soon there was a trail of discarded clothing lying on the floor reaching all the way to Agatha's bed.

Agatha awoke in the grey light of dawn. Memory came flooding back immediately. Her mouth was dry with a raging thirst and her head ached.

She felt lax and immeasurably sad. She had achieved her ambition, her dreams, and got James to take her to bed, but she had not wanted it to be like this, when they were both drunk and hardly knew what they were doing. A tear rolled down one cheek and plopped on the sheet. She twisted round and looked at him. He was sleeping neatly and quietly, his face looking younger in repose.

The worst thing she could now do, she reflected, was to make anything of what had happened. She was old enough and experienced enough to know that James would never even have dreamt of kissing her had he not been extremely drunk. She would need to treat it as everyday, as lightly as she could.

If only she could reach out to him and continue the love-making of the night before. But he might reject her and she could not bear that. She got up, feeling stiff and sore after so much unaccustomed sexual exercise, and went and ran a bath and stayed soaking in it for a long time.

When she returned at last to the bedroom, the bed was empty. James put his head round the door and said, "Just going to have a bath, darling," and went off whistling. He's taking it lightly, thought Agatha, and I must do the same.

She dressed in a blouse and skirt and made her face up carefully, her own face looking strange to her in the mirror.

She then went through to the kitchen and made a cup of coffee and lit a cigarette.

The newspapers plopped through the letter-box and she went to get them. Must cancel these, she thought, and the milk.

James came in as she was reading them. He stooped and kissed her cheek. "Anything about the murder?" he asked.

"Just a bit about Deborah being charged but not much more yet," said Agatha, suddenly shy, not able to look directly at him.

"We'll take the papers along with us and have break-fast outside," he said, "and then we'll get some grapes or something and go and visit Charles. Do you think he'll pay us?"

161

"I didn't think of that," said Agatha. "Should he?"

"Oh, I think so. I mean, we're going to have to pay that farmer for the damage, along with a fine and court costs. If Fraith doesn't offer anything, I'll bill him on behalf of both of us. Coming? You'd better put on a sweater or a jacket or something. It looks a bit chilly."

Agatha went to get a sweater, glad all at once that they were going to have breakfast outside, among people.

As they tucked into bacon and eggs in a hotel dining room, James eyed Agatha across the table. She looked smaller, vulnerable and very withdrawn. She would not meet his eyes. They had been very drunk the night before, admittedly, and he should do the gentlemanly thing and not refer to it, but her passion and generosity had been amazing. Quite amazing. Who would have thought that Agatha, of all people . . .

The thought broke off as Agatha said, "Do you think there'll be anything in the newspapers about us?"

"Not unless the police tell them. We'll be present at the trial as witnesses, so our part in it will come out then."

"Should we phone the papers ourselves?"

He laughed. "Maybe not. Better to keep a low profile. Perhaps we'll make a career or it—Raisin and Lacey, detectives, set up our own bureau of investigation."

Agatha's face lit up. "Why not?"

"Are you serious? I was only joking."

"I don't see why not? We make a good team."

"We'll think about it. Now, if you're finished, let's go and see Charles."

Sir Charles was sitting up in bed at the end of a long ward. His head was bandaged and he looked very white. But he gave a wan smile when he saw them. "Nice to see my saviours," he said. "Isn't it odd that if Deborah hadn't called you in, I'd probably be dead?"

"Very odd," said James, depositing a bag of grapes on the bedside table. "Why aren't you in a private room?"

"Why pay out money when I've been paying taxes all these years?"

James decided in that moment that Charles would not think of giving them any money at all unless they asked for it, so he said, "You'll be getting our bill. Sorry, but it's going to be a bit steep. You see, in our race to rescue you, we damaged some of your neighbour's crops."

"It's all right," said Sir Charles. "Just send it in. The estate agent will see to settling it."

"How are you feeling?" asked Agatha.

"I'm feeling more silly and stupid than anything," said Sir Charles. "Absolutely shiters, in fact. Gustav told me Deborah was creepy. She must have been totally deranged and I never even guessed it. Then my aunt said she was common and that put my back up. I don't like snobbery."

"And yet in a way, it was Deborah's snobbery and ambition that drove her to murder," said James.

"What's that supposed to mean?" Sir Charles peered in the bag and plucked off a grape from the bunch and began to eat it.

"Only that Deborah was determined to be Lady Fraith and run Barfield House," explained James.

Sir Charles looked puzzled. "But it's a nasty building, hardly an architectural gem, more like a glorified farm in a way. Still, it's rather lowering to think it wasn't my delicious body she was after. God, I was stupid. Took her to bed, you know. Awful. Like necrophilia."

163

James had a sudden vivid memory of a fiery and passionate Agatha and blushed dark red.

"Sorry," said Sir Charles, mistaking the reason for the blush. "Always was a bit coarse." He leaned back and closed his eyes.

"Get better soon," said James.

"I will," he said faintly. "As soon as I can get up, I'm off to the south of France for a holiday."

Agatha and James packed up and returned to Carsely that evening, James to his cottage, Agatha to hers. Agatha busied herself with household chores, fed the cats, watered the garden and then went to the Red Lion, trying not to hope that James would be there. But there were only the locals, who talked to her with the sort of half-smiles which told Agatha that she and James going off together had been much discussed and that whatever Mrs. Bloxby had said about them had fallen on deaf ears.

So I've got the reputation of being a fallen woman with none of the pleasure, thought Agatha, and was relieved to escape after a pub meal and get home and go to bed. Before she slipped her nightgown over her head, she stared in the mirror at a naked body which seemed to be slipping back into a sort of spinsterhood, which looked already to her jaundiced eyes as if it had never, ever been made love to.

She took a long time to get to sleep and awoke to find the sun high in the sky and the sound of her doorbell jangling through the house.

She put on her housecoat and ran to answer it, blinking up at the tall figure of James.

"I've got something I want to ask you, Agatha," he

said seriously. And then a voice from a car in the road called, "Coo-ee!"

Agatha peered round him and saw getting out of a little red car her former secretary, Bunty.

"Hi!" said Bunty, walking up to join them. "I was in the area and thought I'd pop in to say hullo."

"Come in," said Agatha wearily to both James and Bunty. She led them into her sitting-room. "I'll go and get coffee," she said.

When she carried in a tray of coffee mugs, Bunty and James were laughing about something, Bunty's fresh young face glowing with health.

All at once Agatha felt so depressed, she thought she would be sick.

She could not bear to sit and watch James being charmed by this young girl, could not bear to have any more evidence that what she had experienced with him was simply a drunken one-night stand.

"I'm awfully sorry," said Agatha, putting down the tray of coffee very carefully on the table, "but I am feeling unwell. I'm sorry, Bunty, but I have got to go and lie down."

"Can I get the doctor?" asked James, alarmed.

"No," said Agatha. "Entertain Bunty for me, would you, James?"

Agatha trailed back to her bedroom, threw her housecoat across the room and crawled back into bed and drew the duvet up over her ears. She was so depressed, she felt she hurt all over. She was nothing but a silly, middle-aged woman.

She dimly heard the door downstairs slam and a car

driving off. They had gone. Maybe they had gone off together for a happy lunch in a pub. Maybe Bunty would ask her to their wedding.

A hand shaking her shoulder made her twist round and stare up.

"Agatha," said James gently. "What's the matter?"

With a great effort, Agatha forced herself to say, "Just a headache, James. If I lie quietly for a bit, I'll be all right."

"Would you like me to bring you some aspirin?"

"No, no. I'll be fine."

He stroked her forehead. "Poor thing. I'll leave you in peace."

"What was it you wanted to talk to me about?" asked Agatha. "The bill for Sir Charles?"

"Oh, that. No." He gave a little laugh. "Of all the times to pick. I actually came round to ask you to marry me, but you'd better get over your headache first before you even think about it."

He turned to walk away.

Agatha sat bolt upright. "Are you joking? What was that about marriage? I mean, *marriage*!"

He came back and sat down on the edge of the bed. "I know you probably like your independence. It hit me last night. We get on very well. The fact is, it all seemed a bit lonely without you. Agatha! What are you doing, Agatha?"

She had started to unbutton his shirt.

"Agatha, what about your headache?"

"What headache?" asked Agatha as she pulled him down on top of her.

An hour later, James said dreamily, "I don't know why, but I seem to remember your telling me that you had walked out on your husband but not divorced him."

Agatha felt a stab of cold fear in her stomach. It had all been so long ago. The last time she had seen Jimmy Raisin had been over thirty years ago, when she left him as he lay in a drunken stupor. He was bound to be dead by now.

She forced herself to laugh. "No, you're mistaken," she said. "Jimmy died of drink ages ago."

"So whose house shall we live in?" he asked. "They're both the same size."

"Yours, I think," said Agatha, promptly forgetting about Jimmy. "You're the one with the most possessions. All those books."

"Did you hear about Mrs. Mason?"

"Oh, her," snorted Agatha. "The cheek of it, telling Deborah I was a phony. What about her?"

"She's devastated about her niece. She's moved off to live with her sister, not Mrs. Camden, another one in Wales, and she's putting her house up for sale. It looks as if the Carsely Ladies Society will be looking for a new chairwoman. Interested?"

"No," said Agatha lazily. "My managing days are over."

"So," said Mrs. Bloxby happily two days later, "I am delighted that both of you are getting married in our church. It will be quite an event for the village. But I was saying to Alf the other day that for some reason I thought you were separated from your husband, not divorced." Alf Bloxby was the vicar.

Again, that stab of fear in Agatha's stomach, but she decided to ignore it and said, "Jimmy's been dead for years." Then she began to worry. Would the vicar expect to see the death certificate? She would need to try to find out what had happened to Jimmy. The wedding was set in three months' time. She and James were seeing a house agent that very afternoon to put Agatha's cottage on the market. She had come such a long way from the days when she had worked as a waitress to support a drunken and increasingly violent husband. The vicarage sitting-room was calm and quiet, with shadows from the sun-dappled leaves in the old garden outside flitting across the walls. Carsely belonged to another world. She refused to think about Jimmy. She was marrying James, and no one was going to stop her.

Bill Wong called that evening just as Agatha was getting ready to go out for dinner with James.

"I saw the announcement of your wedding in the local paper," said Bill. "Congratulations. Have you had a divorce?"

"I don't need a divorce," snapped Agatha. "My husband's dead.

"Agatha, I'm pretty sure you told me you had left him years ago and you didn't know whether he was alive or dead."

"Just because you're a policeman doesn't mean you've got total recall," said Agatha. "You're going to be invited to the wedding, of course."

Bill leaned forward, his features solemn. "Agatha, I'm your friend and I know you well and I know what you feel for James Lacey. Take my advice and get on to a detective agency and get them to trace your husband and find out where he is."

"Are you deaf?" shouted Agatha. "I've told you. He's dead. I'm marrying James Lacey and I'll kill anyone who tries to stop me!"

The next morning, Roy Silver dropped in for a chat with Bunty.

"Haven't you any work to do?" asked Bunty.

"Loads," said Roy cheerfully. "Reluctant to get started, that's all."

"I called on your friend, Agatha Raisin, at the week-end," said Bunty.

"How is the old bat?"

"She wasn't very well. But her fiancé entertained me."

"Her what? I phoned her last night and she said nothing about any engagement."

"Fact. One James Lacey, quite a dish, too. It was in the local paper yesterday. My ma phoned me with the news."

"Well, well," said Roy thoughtfully and drifted off to his own office.

He sat behind his desk and stared into space. He had phoned Agatha at the urging of Mr. Wilson, his boss, who wanted Agatha back. Agatha had been rude and dismissive, had told Roy not to call her again, had told him she was tired of his creepy sycophantic ways, and a few other hard words.

He remembered when he used to work for Agatha's PR firm, Agatha once telling him over a drink that she had walked out on her husband, that she did not know where he was. Of course, that had been some time ago, and maybe Agatha had either heard of her husband's death or divorced him. Still . . .

What a lovely way it would be to pay Agatha back if

169

by any chance she had lied to James and intended to commit bigamy. Would do no harm to find out. He pulled forward the Yellow Pages and began to run his thumb down a list of detective agencies.

The Dembley Walkers trudged out over the countryside. "You know, ah've been thinkin'," said Kelvin, "thon Laceys were an odd couple. Ah think they were working for the police."

"What makes you think that?" asked Mary Trapp.

"It was odd the way they surfaced among us shortly after Jessica's murder and then, when Deborah was arrested, they disappeared."

"I thought that," said Alice. "I'll tell you another thing: That flat they were in in Sheep Street was the property of Sir Charles."

"I could have told you from day one they weren't one of us," said Peter.

"So why didn't you?" jeered Kelvin.

Before Peter could retaliate, a gamekeeper surfaced and told them in no uncertain terms that they were in danger of disturbing the young pheasants. Happily they drew together to meet the challenge. Pheasants were for the rich, the land belonged to all; come the revolution, lackeys like him would be hanging from the nearest lamp-post; and the mysterious Laceys were forgotten.

**Read on for an excerpt from *A Spoonful of Poison*—
the next Agatha Raisin mystery from M. C. Beaton
and St. Martin's / Minotaur Paperbacks!**

Mrs. Bloxby, wife of the vicar of Carsely, looked nervously at her visitor. "Yes, Mrs. Raisin is a friend of mine, a very dear friend, but she is now very busy running her detective agency and does not have spare time for—"

"But this is such a good cause," interrupted Arthur Chance, vicar of Saint Odo The Severe in the village of Comfrey Magna. "The services of an expert public relations officer to bring the crowds to our annual fête would be most welcome. Proceeds will go to restore the church roof and to various charities."

"Yes, but—"

"It would do no harm to just *ask,* now would it? It is your Christian duty."

"I hardly need to be reminded of my duty," said Mrs. Bloxby wearily, thinking of all the parish visits, the mothers' meetings and the Carsely Ladies' Society. Really, she thought, surveying the vicar, for such a mild, inoffensive-looking man he is terribly pushy. Arthur Chance was a small man with thick glasses and grey hair which stuck out in tufts like horns on either side of his creased and wrinkled face. He had married a woman twenty years his junior, Mrs. Bloxby remembered. He probably bullied her into it, she thought.

"Look! I will do what I can, but I cannot promise anything. When is the fête?"

"It is a week on Saturday."

"Only about a week away. You are not giving Mrs. Raisin any time."

"God will help her," said Mr. Chance.

Agatha Raisin, a middle-aged woman who had sold up her successful public relations business to take early retirement in a cottage in the Cotswolds, had found that inactivity did not suit her and so had started up her own private detective agency. Now that it was successful, however, she wished she had more time to relax. Also, the cases which poured into the detective agency all concerned messy divorces, missing children, missing cats and dogs, and only the occasional case of industrial espionage. She had begun to close the agency at weekends, feeling she was losing quality time, forgetting that when she had plenty of quality time, she didn't know what to do with it.

For a woman in her early fifties, she still looked well. Her hair, although tinted, was glossy and her legs good. Although she had small eyes, she had very few wrinkles. She had a generous bosom and a rather thick waist, which was her despair.

On Friday evening, when she arrived home, she fussed over her two cats, Hodge and Boswell, kicked off her shoes, mixed herself a generous gin and tonic, lit a cigarette, and lay back on the sofa with a sigh of relief.

She wondered idly where her ex-husband, James Lacey, was. He lived next door to her but worked as a travel writer and was often abroad. She rummaged around in her brain as usual, searching for that old obsession, that old longing for him, but it seemed to have gone forever. Agatha, without an obsession, was left with herself; and she forgot about all the pain and misery that obsession for her ex had brought and remembered only the brief bursts of elation.

The doorbell shrilled. Agatha swung her legs off the sofa and went to answer the door. Her face lit up when she saw Mrs. Bloxby standing there. "Come in," she cried. "I'm just having a G and T. Want one?"

"No, but I'd like a sherry."

Sometimes Agatha, often too aware of her slum upbringing, wondered what it would be like to be a lady inside and out like Mrs. Bloxby. The vicar's wife was wearing a rather baggy tweed skirt and a rose-pink blouse which had seen better days. Her grey hair was escaping from a bun at the back of her neck, but she had her usual air of kindness and dignity.

The pair of them, as was the fashion in the Carsely Ladies' Society, always called each other by their second names.

Agatha poured Mrs. Bloxby a sherry. "I haven't seen you for a while," said Agatha. "It's been so busy."

A brief flicker of guilt crossed Mrs. Bloxby's grey eyes. "Have you still got that young detective with you, Toni Gilmour?"

"Yes, thank goodness. Excellent worker. But I think we will need to start turning down cases. I really don't want to take on more staff."

Mrs. Bloxby took a sip of sherry and said distractedly, "I knew you would be too busy. That's what I told him."

"Told who?"

"Mr. Arthur Chance. The vicar of Saint Odo The Severe."

"The what?"

"An Anglo-Saxon saint. I forget what he did. There are so many of them."

"So how did my name come up in your discussion with Mr. Chance?"

"He lives in Comfrey Magna—"

"Never been there."

"Few people have. It's off the tourist route. Anyway, they are having their annual village fête a week tomorrow and Mr. Chance wanted me to beg you to publicize the event for them."

"Is there anything special about this vicar? Any reason why I should?"

"Only because it's for charity. And he is rather pushy."

Agatha smiled. "You look like a woman who has just been bullied. Tell you what, we'll drive over there tomorrow morning and I will tell him one resounding *no* and he won't bother you again."

"That is so good of you, Mrs. Raisin. I am not very strong when it comes to saying no to good works."

In the winter days, when the rain dripped down and thick wet fog covered the hills, Agatha sometimes wondered what she was doing buried under the thatch of her cottage in the Cotswolds.

But as she drove off with Mrs. Bloxby the following morning, the countryside was enjoying a really warm spring. Blackthorn starred the hedgerows, wisteria and clematis hung on garden walls, bluebells shook in the

174

lightest of breezes, and a large blue sky arched over-head.

Mrs. Bloxby guided Agatha through a maze of country lanes. "Here we are at last," she said finally. "Just park in front of the church."

Agatha thought Comfrey Magna was an odd, secretive-looking village. There were no new houses to mar the straggling line of ancient cottages on either side of the road. She could see no one on the main street or in the gardens or even at the windows.

"Awfully quiet," she commented.

"Few young people, that's the problem," said Mrs. Bloxby. "No first-time buyers, only last-time buyers."

"Shouldn't think houses would be all that expensive in a dead hole like this," said Agatha, parking the car.

"Houses all over are dreadfully expensive."

They got out of the car. "That's the vicarage over there," said Mrs. Bloxby. "We'll cut through the churchyard."

The vicarage was an old grey building with a sloping roof of old Cotswold tiles, the kind that cost a fortune but that the local council would never allow anyone to sell, unless they were going to be replaced with exactly the same thing, which, of course, defeated the purpose.

As they entered the churchyard, Agatha saw a man straightening up from one of the graves where he had been laying flowers. He turned and saw them and smiled.

Agatha blinked rapidly. He was tall, with fair hair, a lightly tanned handsome face, and green eyes. His eyes were really green, thought Agatha, not a fleck of brown in them. He was wearing a tweed sports jacket and cavalry-twill trousers.

"Good morning," said Mrs. Bloxby pleasantly, but

giving Agatha's arm a nudge because that lady seemed to have become rooted to the spot.

"Good morning," he replied.

"Who was that?" whispered Agatha as they approached the door of the vicarage.

"I don't know."

Mrs. Bloxby rang the bell. The door was opened by a tall woman wearing a leotard and nothing else. Her hair was tinted aubergine and worn long and straight. She had rather mean features—a narrow, thin mouth and long narrow eyes. Her nose was thin with an odd bump in the middle, as if it had once been broken and then badly reset. Pushing forty, thought Agatha.

"You've interrupted my Pilates exercises," she said.

"We've come to see Mr. Chance," said Mrs. Bloxby.

"You must be the PR people. You'll find him in the study. I'm Trixie Chance."

Oh dear, thought Mrs. Bloxby. She often thought that trendy vicars' wives did as much to reduce a church congregation as a trendy vicar. Mrs. Chance was of a type familiar to her: always desperately trying to be "cool," following the latest fads and quoting the names of the latest pop groups.

Trixie had disappeared. By pushing open a couple of doors off the hall, they found the study. Arthur Chance was sitting behind a large Victorian desk piled high with papers.

He rushed round the desk to meet them, his pale eyes shining behind thick glasses. He seized Agatha's hands. "Dear lady, I knew you would come. How splendid of you to help us!"

Agatha disengaged her hands. "I have come here," she began, "to say—"

There was a trill of laughter from outside, and through the window Agatha could see Trixie talking to that handsome man.

"Who is that man?" she demanded, pointing at the window.

Arthur swung round in surprise. "Oh, that is one of my parishioners, Mr. George Selby. So tragic, his wife dying like that! He has been a source of strength helping me with the organization of the fête, ordering the marquees in case it rains. So important in our fickle English climate, don't you think, Mrs. Raisin?"

"Certainly," gushed Agatha. "Perhaps, if you could call Mr. Selby in, we could discuss the publicity together?"

"Certainly, certainly." Arthur bustled off. Mrs. Bloxby stifled a sigh. She knew her friend was now dead set on another romantic pursuit. She wished, not for the first time, that Agatha would grow up.

George Selby entered the study behind the vicar. He smiled at Agatha. "Are you sure you want to do this?" he asked. "Mr. Chance can be very persuasive."

"It's no trouble at all," said Agatha, thinking she should have worn a pair of heels instead of the dowdy flat sandals she was wearing.

But Agatha's heart sank as the events were described to her. There was to be entertainment by the village band and dancing by a local group of morris men. The rest consisted of competitions to see who had created the best cake, bread, pickles, and relishes. The main event was the home-made jam tasting.

She sat in silence after the vicar had finished outlining the events. She caught a sympathetic look from George's beautiful green eyes and a great idea leaped into her mind.

"Yes, I can do this," she said. "You haven't given me much time. Leave it to me." She turned to George. "Perhaps we could have dinner sometime in the coming week to discuss progress?"

He hesitated slightly. "Splendid idea," said the vicar. "Plan our campaign. There is a very good restaurant at Mircester. Trixie, my wife, is particularly fond of it. La Belle Cuisine. Why don't we all meet there for dinner on Wednesday? Eight o'clock."

"Fine," said Agatha gloomily.

"I suppose so," said George with a marked lack of enthusiasm.

Agatha's staff, consisting of detectives Phil Marshall, Patrick Mulligan, young Toni Gilmour and secretary Mrs. Freedman, found that the usual Monday-morning conference was cancelled. "Just get on with whatever you're on with," said Agatha. "I've got a church fête to sell."

Toni felt low. She had been given another divorce case and she hated divorce cases. But she lingered in the office, fascinated to hear Agatha Raisin in full bullying mode on the phone. "Yes, I think you should send a reporter. We're running a real food campaign here. Good home-village produce and no supermarket rubbish. And I can promise you a surprise. Yes, it *is* Agatha Raisin here. No, no murder, hah, hah. Just send a reporter."

Next call. "I want to speak to Betsy Wilson."

Toni stood frozen. Betsy Wilson was a famous pop singer. "Tell her it's Agatha Raisin. Hullo, Betsy, dear, remember me? I want you to open a village fête next Saturday. I know you have a busy schedule, but I also happen to know you are between gigs. The press will all be there. Good for your image. Lady-of-the-manor bit. Large hat, floaty dress, gracious—come on, girl, by the time I'm finished with you I'll have you engaged to Prince William. Yes, you come along and I'll see if I can get the prince." Agatha then charged on to tell Betsy to arrive at two o'clock and to give her directions to Comfrey Magna.

"Thick as two planks," muttered Agatha, "but she's coming."

"But she's famous!" gasped Toni. "Why should she come?"

"Her career was sinking after that drugs bust," said Agatha. "I did a freelance job and got her going again."

She picked up the phone again. "News desk? Forget about the healthy food. Better story. Fête is to be opened by Betsy Wilson. Yes. I thought that would make you sit up."

Toni waited until Agatha had finished the call and asked, "Can you really get Prince William?"

"Of course not, but that dumb cow thinks I'm capable of anything."

* * * *

Agatha sustained a visit from a very angry Bill Wong on Friday evening. "You might have told me first what your plans were," he complained, "and I would have done my best to stop you. Betsy Wilson! It's as bad as hiring Celine Dion for the occasion."

He was only slightly mollified by the news that Agatha had engaged a security firm that had promised to put as many of their men as possible on the ground.

Bill was the product of a Chinese father and a Gloucestershire mother. He had inherited his father's almond-shaped eyes, those eyes which were looking suspiciously at Agatha. "Who is he?" asked Bill.

"He? Who?"

"You've fallen for someone."

"Bill, can you not for once believe something good about me? I'm doing this for charity."

"So you say. I'll be there myself on Saturday."

"How's your love life?" countered Agatha. "Still dating my young detective, Toni Gilmour?"

"We go around together when we both get some free time, but . . ."

"But what?"

"Agatha, could you try to find out what she thinks of me? Toni is very affectionate and likes me, but there's no spark there, no hint of passion. Mother and Father like her a lot."

Agatha eyed him shrewdly. "You know, Bill, you can't go after a girl just because your mother and father like her. Do you *yearn* for her?"

"Don't be embarrassing."

"All right. I'll find out what her intentions are."

"I'd better go. See you tomorrow."

Agatha, who had been sitting on a kitchen chair, rose with one fluid movement to show him out.

"You've had a hip replacement!" exclaimed Bill.

"Nonsense. It wasn't arthritis after all. A pulled muscle."

Agatha had no intention of telling Bill or anybody else that she had paid one thousand pounds at the Nuffield Hospital in Cheltenham for a hip injection. The surgeon had warned her that she would soon have to have a hip replacement, but now, free of pain, Agatha forgot his words. Arthritis was so ageing. She was sure it had been a pulled muscle.

George Selby had to admit to himself that it looked as if the day was going to be a success. Betsy Wilson was a rare pop singer in that she appealed to families as well as teenagers. He also had to admit that had she not arrived to open the fête, only a few people would have attended. What was considered the height of the fête was the tasting to find the best home-made jam. Little dishes of jam were laid out, and people tasted each and then dropped a note of their favourite in a ballot box.

The sun shone from a cloudless sky on the beauty of spring. It had been a cold, damp early spring, and now, with the sudden heat and good weather, it seemed as if everything had blossomed at once: cherry and lilac, wisteria and hawthorn and all the glory of the fruit trees in the orchards around the village.

Betsy Wilson, in a gauzy dress decorated with roses, made a short speech, clasped her hands and sang her latest hit, "Every Other Sunday." It was a haunting ballad. Her clear young voice floated up to the Cotswold hills. Even the hardened pressmen stood silently.

She sang two more ballads, finished by singing "Amazing Grace," and then was hustled into a stretch limo by her personal security guard. The band which had accompanied her packed up and left, to be replaced by the village band.

Then Toni, who was with Agatha, tugged her sleeve and said, "That's odd."

"What's odd?" asked Agatha.

"Look at all those teenagers queuing outside the jam tent."

"Really? If I thought it was going to be such a popular event, I'd have charged an extra admission fee."

"Could someone be peddling drugs inside that tent?" asked Toni.

"Why?"

"Some of the people coming out look stoned."

Agatha was about to walk towards the tent when she heard screams and commotion coming from over by the church. People were pointing upwards. A woman was standing at the top of the square Norman tower, her arms outstretched. As Agatha ran over to the church, followed by Toni, she heard someone say, "It's old Mrs. Andrews. Her said something about how her could fly."

Agatha saw George running into the church and ran after him, with Toni pounding after her. George was disappearing through a door at the back of the church where stairs led to the tower. Agatha ran up the stairs, panting and gasping as she neared the top. She staggered out onto the roof.

Mrs. Andrews was standing up on the parapet. "I can fly," she said dreamily. "Just like Superman."

George made a lunge for her—but too late.

With an odd little laugh, Mrs. Andrews sailed straight off into space. George, Agatha and Toni craned their heads over the parapet. Mrs. Andrews lay smashed on a table tombstone, a pool of dark blood spreading from her head.

George was white-faced. "What on earth came over her? She was a perfectly sane woman."

"The jam," said Toni suddenly. "I think someone's put something in the jam."

"Get down there," said Agatha, "and tell the security guards to seal off that damned tent."

She was about to run after Toni when George caught her arm. "What's this about the jam?"

"Toni noticed that an awful lot of teenagers were queuing up outside the jam tent and coming out looking stoned. I've got to get down there."

When they arrived outside the church, a woman came up to them looking distraught. "Get an ambulance. Old Mrs. Jessop's jumped into the river."

Police were beginning to shout through loudhailers that everyone was to stay exactly where they were until interviewed.

"Thousands of them," gasped Toni. "I *told* Bill there was something wrong with the jam."